I Only Made Up the Roses

I Only Made Up the Roses

by Barbara Ann Porte

GREENWILLOW BOOKS New York

Portions of Chapters 1 and 2 appeared in
considerably different form as stories in
Green's Magazine, Canada (Winter 1985)
and in *San Jose Studies* (Winter 1986/87).

Printed in the United States of America
First Edition

10 9 8 7 6 5 4 3 2 1

Library of Congress
Cataloging-in-Publication Data

Porte, Barbara Ann.
I only made up the roses.
Summary: Seventeen-year-old Cydra
presents a portrait of her family
whose history spans three continents.
[1. Family life—Fiction.
2. Afro-Americans—Fiction]   I. Title.
PZ7.P7995Io 1987   [Fic]   86-18307
ISBN 0-688-05216-9

for my husband's parents, with love,
for HELEN CLARK THOMAS
and in memory of
P. FLOYD THOMAS

Contents

Children's children are the crown of old men;
and the glory of children are their fathers.

—PROVERBS, 17:6

I Only Made Up the Roses

1 🦢
The Funeral

THAT same spring when I, Cydra, turned seventeen, 250,000 chickens in Virginia keeled over dead from heat prostration, and Granddad, who was out in back behind his house, feeding the dozen or so that he still kept, had his first and final heart attack. His funeral was three days later.

It conveys no disrespect to say that Granddad and chickens have often been connected in my mind. One of the first stories I ever heard that I remember was one that Granddad told me about chickens. He had grown up on a farm. Helping his mother and grandmother pluck them was one of his first chores. After they'd been plucked, he explained, his mother would singe the pinfeathers off.

"The first time I heard her," he said, "I thought she said, 'Sing, sing the pinfeathers off.' For years and years afterward I carried in my head a picture of my mother and my grandmother, a plucked chicken held between them, both of them singing until its final feathers fell out." Since I heard him tell it, I, too, have held that picture in my head.

By the time I knew him, Granddad no longer had any connection with a farm, but he raised brooders as a hobby. He raised them far enough away from the large stone house, which he and Grandmother had built and lived in, so that she could not complain about their sight or sound or smell. They owned that much land, and more beyond it.

The family is gathered now in this room where I am standing, in the funeral home where Granddad's body is laid out. Daddy stands beside me, Mother is on his other side, and Perley, my brother, is in front, leaning against me, scuffing one shoe with his other as he is not supposed to do. Perley is nine. Like everybody else in this room of relatives, except for Mother and me, Perley is black, though in the color-coded world we live, black can be a shade as light as sand, and I have cousins whose skin is fairer than my own.

I listen as Aunt Selena asks Aunt Sister which tie would be better, the blue one or the black one. The blue one, they decide. If everyone would just be quieter, that would be much better, I think. I look at my father. My father is quiet. He is a quiet person who does not believe in noise, or talk, or chatter, as he most often calls what they are doing. Running their mouths, he says; the problem with most folks is that they talk too much. I think he also does not really believe in what is right this minute going on. My father is not one to favor ceremony. I hear Grandmother from the corner of the room, where she is arranging with the funeral director for flowers, a photographer, and the coffin to be taken to the house, where Granddad will remain until his funeral.

"The only man I know of," Cousin Tineen will say later, "to go from his own living room, out his own front door, to attend his own funeral." I watch my father carefully as he stands unmoving. Only the pressure of his hand on mine lets me know that he is taking note of everything that's going on.

Afterward, back at the house, Grandmother's house now, I think, we move furniture, preparing the living room to accommodate the coffin. We remove the large armchair in which Granddad used to sit, leaned back and comfortable, making that corner seem the center of the room. He sat there, though, only when it was too hot or cold to sit outside or late at night. Outside was the place that he liked best, at the picnic table where no one ever had a picnic I knew of, underneath the old magnolia tree. There almost always is a breeze. In New York, where I was born and spent my first ten years, few people know magnolia trees will grow so tall as that one. They call tulip trees magnolias, dwarfed though they are. Trees that short, I guess, can stand the cold. Virginia trees don't have to.

When I was Perley's age, whenever we visited, I'd squeeze myself against that tree or underneath the table or a bench, hoping to avoid attention, and listen to Granddad and his friends tell stories. The first time I heard about wild dogs in the country was at the picnic table. They fed them sponges, soaked first in bacon grease.

"Lard-drenched sponges left out overnight," Granddad said, "will cure you of wild dogs." The second time I heard about the wild dog remedy was in English class last year, when we read a group of stories by a southern writer. So, I thought, it was true after all. Then I felt ashamed for being quicker to believe a stranger's writing than what my own grandfather said.

Wild dogs were in Alabama when Granddad was starting out, working for the old Farm Bureau. "Department of Agriculture we call it now," he'd explain in his soft voice, saying each syllable separately, smiling as if he were telling a joke.

Anytime I hear Alabama mentioned, I pay attention. Daddy was born in Alabama. He lived there until he was twelve. "Twelve years in Alabama," he'll say, "is as much as anyone should have to spend." It is not a place he ever thinks of going back to visit.

One of his first memories is of playing outside in his front yard, digging in the dirt. When he looked up, there was a rifle pointed at his head. It was held by a person dressed in white, white sheet, white shoes, white hood.

"What did that person say?" I once asked. Father smiled at me, his downturned smile I always take to mean the opposite of smile.

"I didn't wait to hear," he answered.

Daddy's parents both were born in Alabama and grew up there. They didn't meet until they went to college in Michigan. They returned to Alabama to get married and to start their family. They taught school, bought land, built houses, sold or rented them. It financed their children's private education. If degrees are any measure, the children all did well. Aunt Sister has a Ph.D. in anthropology. Daddy's degree is in engineering. Uncle William is a lawyer. And Aunt Selena is working on her third master's, this one in Egyptology. "She never could make up her mind about anything," Grandmother has said in criticism. All of them also deal at least part of the time in real estate.

My father calls to me to ride to the cemetery with him. Again I listen as they make arrangements. Grandfather will be laid to rest in a box with his name on it inside one of two mausoleums on the grounds. The children will have keys for when they visit. If it were left to me, I would bury Granddad out-of-doors, in his own side yard underneath the tall magnolia tree. Well, I know it's not allowed. A person cannot be buried in a garden; there are health department rules.

"You know," Grandmother points out to me going home, "that is the only cemetery in this town. If someone were to open up a second cemetery," she continues, "that person could do a fine business." Grandmother is not one to let a lesson pass a grandchild by no matter what the circumstances.

I nod and answer only, "Yes, ma'am." I consider, though, how not so long ago there would have had to be two cemeteries anyway, a black one and a white one. It crosses my mind to wonder if one mausoleum houses only dead white bodies and the other black. Probably not, I think; no one would know, there'd be no point. But then I see that is the point. If no one knows, *they* still can do exactly as they like. Besides, there never was a point, and *they* did as they liked.

Granddad is in the living room when we get home, wearing the clothes my aunts picked out. He is dressed the way he always dressed. Anytime you saw him he had on a white shirt and a tie, and a jacket at least within reaching distance. My father is the same way when it comes to dressing, and so is Uncle William. The house is filled with people. It will be that way all day, into the evening and all of tomorrow.

The ladies from the church have set up a coffee urn and platters of food in the dining room, chicken and greens, biscuits and ham, and sweet potato pies. How everyone can eat with Granddad lying in the next room dead, I do not understand. But even my father is eating, and then everyone is moving through the house, in one door and out the other. Everyone is shaking hands and taking turns standing by the casket. Grandmother has them sign a guest book before they leave. I think how it looks much more like a wedding than it does a wake, but having never been to either one before, I have no way of really knowing. I overhear Aunt Sister say that Mother, meaning Grandmother, was correct after all. She means correct about the body staying in the house. It seems there was some talk about it. "Yes," Aunt Selena answers, "I think it's helping everyone adjust." I wonder who it's helping. Can it be helping me? I watch my father shaking hands and wonder if it's helping him. Then I think there can be no adjusting to such news, nor should there be, that a person whom you love can stand in front of you, or take a walk, be sitting just outside, and disappear forever. I recall a story that I read last year. It was about a young woman married to an older man, a writer. Every day she sought to keep her aging husband safe. She would not go mountain climbing with him, or allow him to go alone, for fear he'd have a heart attack. Nor did she permit him to travel in an airplane, even on a business trip, for fear of accident. He died asleep one night in their double bed. It was the one possibility she had forgotten to consider, that he could die by her side despite her best precautions. I decide to try to keep in mind forever every possibility.

It is past midnight now, and except for the relatives staying overnight, which we are, most of the rest have gone home. We live on the Virginia side of Washington, D.C. It is a three-hour drive south to Grandmother's house, too far to go home and come back. A neighbor says in a low voice to Uncle William as she leaves, "Leave the door open tonight." I wonder if she is thinking of ghosts. But then I see she means to keep it cool. Even this early in the spring Virginia has been sweltering all week in a heat wave. Even with embalming fluid in his veins, there is concern about decomposition. I do not care to think about it. I close my eyes and picture Granddad outside underneath his tree. There is a cool breeze blowing. "Hey there, Cyd," he calls to me. "How are you doing?"

Morning comes; relatives who left have returned. Some of the great-aunts and great-uncles have stayed up all night beside Granddad. There is no point in my complaining I am tired.

Grandmother is dressed for the funeral entirely in black with a hat and a veil. She looks more beautiful than I have ever seen her look. It is easy to see where my aunts' own good looks have come from. The stern expression that she almost always wears has been replaced by sadness. Daddy bends over and tells her softly that it is time to leave for church. Grandmother rises.

"William," she calls. "William," she says as she used to. She is calling to Granddad to tell him it is time to leave, time to leave for his funeral, time to start out for church. Then it comes to her what she is doing, how he won't be there forever to be called. Her body slumps, as though while I am watching, it has gotten smaller. Aunt Sister puts an arm around her and helps her through the doorway, down the steps. We get into the cars as the coffin is being removed from the house.

When we arrive at the church, it seems that half the town must be inside, the other half outside for lack of space. Grandmother disengages herself from Aunt Sister's helping arm and starts to give directions. Seeing work to be done, she visibly grows stronger. She tells us where to sit. She says who'll drive which car and in what order following the church ceremony, going to the cemetery. She discusses how to manage traffic with the police escort she prearranged. Finally she nods. We're ready to begin.

The service is simple and solemn and moving. A man I do not know, a family friend, sings in a heartbreaking tenor

Granddad's favorite hymn, "May the Work That I Have Done Speak for Me." The minister says more than once, "He has overcome the world." I like to think that it is so.

Afterward we go to the cemetery, back to the church to eat, then to Grandmother's house, where we plan to stay at least another day. At church I eat only a little. I would not eat at all except I worry my cousins will think that I am showing off. But later, alone in Grandmother's kitchen, I find I am hungry. I start to eat slowly; then, suddenly, with no warning, I am stuffing myself as fast as I can with leftover biscuits and yesterday's ham and finishing up with homemade vanilla ice cream, which I spoon from the bucket into my mouth with no plate between. It occurs to me to wonder if Granddad made the ice cream. He usually did. Who will make homemade ice cream anymore?

I go outside and sit down at the empty picnic table underneath the tree. After a while Perley comes and joins me. Then Grandmother comes, too, and sits down across from us. She is not wearing a wig. She has taken off the wig that she has worn every day since I have known her, except for times when she was sleeping. I like the way she looks without it, her short gray hair like a feathery cap on her head, softening her expression.

Now, and in the days to come, I wonder what it means that she has given up her wig. If you knew my grandmother, though, you would know it is not a question anyone would ever ask her. We sit that way a few more minutes; then Perley gets up to go inside. Noticing my hesitation, Grandmother tells me to go on ahead. "I'd just as soon," she says, "sit here by myself awhile."

Daddy and Mother are side by side on the couch in Grandmother's sitting room when we go in. Daddy has hardly let Mother out of his sight since we heard the news. She is still dressed in the black skirt she wore to the funeral, bought just before we left to come here and too long, a black quilted jacket, and black pumps she borrowed this morning from Aunt Selena when she realized the brown ones she brought wouldn't do.

Daddy looks up as we enter. His shoulders droop, his hands are splayed in his lap. There is a lost look in his eyes. He has aged even in the short time since his father died, more than I would have believed possible. Almost as if he'd read my mind, he says in his soft way, "Now I am the older generation," and I am struck for the first time by how a person comes to that position.

2 🙶

The Farm

SEVERAL years ago Daddy took us to visit his uncle Ben on his farm in South Carolina. Uncle Ben was Granddad's youngest brother. Daddy had spent his own summers when he was growing up on his grandfather's farm.

"The bees were the worst part," he said. His grandmother had kept bees for honey. "I lived every summer in fear of an attack."

I already knew about attack bees from my aunt Alice, Mother's sister, though in her case they actually were hornets.

"Bees, hornets—when they attack, you hardly notice any difference," said Aunt Alice. I'm sure she was right. At the time she said it she was living in the country. Having decided to change her life-style, she had sublet her apartment in Manhattan and bought some acres in rural New

York, north of Albany. She lived in a trailer on the land with three cats, a dog, and a goat. She bought the goat thinking it would eat the grass and she wouldn't have to mow it. "Being a farmer," she said to my mother, "is one thing; cutting grass is another." The goat apparently agreed. It never ate the grass that anybody knew about; instead, it climbed onto her picnic table, and it ate her trees.

One day, when Aunt Alice was out back trying to discourage it, she disturbed a hornet's nest, and all of them came after her. She told us about it, of course, after the fact: how she had run for the trailer, the dog at her heels, shedding her hornet-filled clothes as she went, arriving in the kitchen totally naked except for her feet, removing her sneakers and shaking hornets from her socks. Mother could never understand the calm with which Aunt Alice told us this.

"It makes me hysterical," she said, "just to hear it." Perley wanted to know about the goat. Aunt Alice had given it away, but that wasn't what he meant.

"Did the hornets sting the goat, too?" Perley persisted.

"I certainly hope so," said Aunt Alice.

Eventually she sold her land and moved back to the city. "Country life," she said, "may be fine for a farmer, but it was a bit too much excitement for me."

Father felt just that way, too, especially concerning bees. In his case, whenever he had gone to town for his grandmother, and that was at least once a week, he had to ride the mule over the hill and straight through the place where the beehives were kept.

"It was the worst experience of my life," he said. "What made it even worse was knowing that I would have to pass the same way coming home and that even if I made it safely there and back, the entire trip would have to be repeated the following week and the week after that and the week after that for the rest of my summers so far as I knew, or until I was dead from bee stings." Why he couldn't have found an alternate route was something I didn't understand. "There was no other route," he insisted. "Of course, it did have its good side."

"Oh," Mother asked, "what was that?"

"Nothing I ever had to do again," he explained, "seemed half so bad."

Mother, who was raised in the city, liked to think of herself as a country person at heart. "I should have been born on a farm," she frequently said. Father, always grateful that he wasn't, tried to tell her she had no idea what living on a farm was like. I think it was mostly to give her some idea that he planned our trip that weekend to Uncle Ben's farm.

"Pack farm clothes," he said at the time. Mother had no problem. She is an artist who wears farm clothes when she works. Dungarees and sweatshirts are the mainstay of her wardrobe. Perley put his cowboy boots and hat into a shopping bag.

"We're going to a farm," I told him, "not a ranch."

"Perley has the right idea," said Father, watching. "If I were you," he said to me as I prepared to pack my sandals, "I'd take something more substantial for my feet. I can tell," he said, "you haven't spent much time around a cow barn." Daddy, as usual, wore a three-piece suit and a tie. We drove to the farm.

"What are your aunt and uncle like?" I asked on the way. Daddy couldn't remember.

"I haven't seen Aunt Reesa since I was ten," he told me. "I remember she had hair long enough that she could sit on it. I thought that she looked ghostly."

"Ghostly?" I wondered if he meant ghastly.

"She was extremely thin," said Daddy.

Meeting her, I saw that she still was. Also, she looked white. "Creole," Daddy told me, "her people were from New Orleans." None of them, not even Uncle Ben, turned out to look like Daddy, who is tall, broad-shouldered, and dark. They were a family of small people, very slender, with finely chiseled features. The children and the grand-children especially showed abundant evidence of their Indian, French, and African ancestry.

"Indian," I said in second grade when I first knew, "my father is part Indian."

"What kind of Indian?" my teacher asked, interested.

"Blackfoot," I answered. "I think he is Blackfoot." It was only last year that Perley informed me that the name Blackfoot comes from the color members of that tribe dyed their moccasins. Perley can be counted on for information like that. When he started school, he begged for an encyclopedia. Mother and Daddy bought him a set for Christmas, and ever since he has been reading it.

The same day we arrived I overheard Cousin Thera say to my father, "It was that summer when they burned the cross on our lawn, and afterward Mother didn't care to travel anymore with Daddy." I was surprised to hear her measure time the same way that he does, using personal events for markers. Later I asked him about the traveling part.

"Well," he said, "a person only looking at Aunt Reesa wouldn't know she wasn't white. It made traveling rather tricky in the South."

The farm was a lot smaller than I expected, having seen pictures before only of Iowa and Kansas corn and wheatfields, which seemed to stretch as far as one's eye could see. Uncle Ben's farm could be taken in in one eyeful. He did not grow corn or wheat. What he grew mainly were a few sheep, some cows, and lots of chickens. The cows were not for milking.

"What are they for then?" Perley asked, reaching through the bars to pet them. No one seemed anxious to tell him. I certainly didn't plan to, but what I did instead I must say took me by surprise. I reached through the bars as Perley had to pet the cows. Then I felt my fingers, unplanned, moving on their own, search out that special spot on the nearest cow's head, the sledgehammer-shaped spot between and under its eyes, above its mouth, that I knew about from Daddy. I knew about it from the time he'd mentioned he once had shot a pig on the farm when he was a boy.

"Why?" I asked. "Why did you shoot a pig?"

"Don't be silly," Mother said. "He's only teasing."

"It was how we killed them," Daddy told me.

"Sure, killed them," said Mother, "but why would someone send a child out with a gun to shoot a pig when there were plenty of grown men around to do it? Why didn't your grandfather or one of your uncles shoot the pig?"

"Maybe," I said, trying to be helpful, "they were busy shooting the cows."

"We didn't shoot cows," said Father.

"Why was that?" Mother asked.

"A cow," Father explained, "was killed with a sledge-hammer blow."

"I see," Mother said, then changed the topic.

Days went by before I could bring myself to ask what I wanted to know. "Why weren't the pigs killed with a sledgehammer, too?"

"Because," Father told me gently, "there is no sledge-hammer-shaped place on a pig's head as there is on a cow's."

There on the farm I knew for the first time precisely what he meant. I was touching a spot that certainly seemed ready-made for a sledgehammer blow. I petted the cow and thought sorrowfully how much better off she might be without it.

"Do you have any pigs?" Perley asked.

"Last year I had one pig," Uncle Ben told him, "but I don't have it anymore." I wondered, but did not ask him, if he had shot it.

A few minutes later I saw Perley tug at Daddy's sleeve. Daddy bent down, and Perley whispered something to him. I saw a look of astonishment cross Daddy's face, but whatever he answered back I wasn't close enough to hear.

"Did you ask about the wild boar?" I asked Perley

suspiciously the minute I got him alone. The week before we had watched a show together on educational television. The narrator had said with great enthusiasm that of all the interesting things to know about a wild pig, more interesting even than its foot-long tusks or versatile snout, was that the male pig's sex organ was eighteen inches long with a corkscrew at its end that could be twirled around and around during mating. At the time Perley probably didn't even know what mating was, but the part about the corkscrew really captured his attention. He tried to look it up, but his encyclopedia didn't mention it. Nor was his the sort of question he could ask a reference librarian. What Perley wanted to know, and had tried to find out, was if farm pigs and wild pigs had everything the same. "What did Daddy say?" I asked him. Perley looked disappointed.

"He said that he had no idea." Perley did know a pig joke, however, and shared it with me. This was his joke:

A man in a car with a pig was stopped by the police.

"What are you doing with a pig in your car?" he was asked.

"We're going for a ride," said the man.

"Pigs are not allowed in town." The policeman told him to take it to the zoo.

"I'll do that," said the man.

Next week: same man, same pig, same car.

"I thought I told you," the policeman said, stopping him, "to take that pig to the zoo."

"I did," said the man. "He had such a good time I'm taking him back."

"Cute," I told Perley, who couldn't stop laughing. He

always thinks his jokes are a riot. No one ever has the heart to tell him otherwise.

"Chickens," Uncle Ben told us next morning as Perley and I stooped down and followed him into the chicken house to help collect the eggs, "will sometimes eat their own eggs if they're not collected soon enough." I was surprised to hear it. "Well," he said, "not every chicken will do that, but the ones that do it will do it regularly. When your father was your age," he told Perley, "he sometimes had to help wring the chickens' necks on the farm. Your aunt Sister cried so hard the time they tried to make her do it they never tried again.

"Once," he said, "a hired man on our farm went to ax a chicken. He crossed its wings so they wouldn't flap, laid its head against the tree stump, and stepped on the chicken's feet with his own to hold them down. But when he swung the ax, it hit against a pole, bounced back, and cut off his nose. My mother, your great-grandmother, picked up the nose, cleaned it off, and sewed it right back on that hired man's face with black thread she kept in a box for sewing up the animals."

When we got back to the house, I asked Aunt Reesa what she did with all the eggs.

"Ben sells them," she told me, by her manner disassociating herself from the business end of it. "Ben's farm" was how she referred to the land and animals that surrounded the house where they lived. She seemed to prefer staying inside or outside on the porch, swinging in the lawn swing.

The walls inside the house were almost completely covered over by photographs of the children and grand-children; in between the photographs were crayon draw-ings that some of them had made and school pa-pers, certificates, and newspaper clippings. Some were from decades ago; others were recent. Wherever you looked there were knickknacks, and an antique doll collec-tion surrounded the fireplace. Kerosene stoves were in all of the rooms, and there was an abundance of quilts. "One year," Aunt Reesa told Mother, who was admiring them, "I made thirty-four altogether." She got up and went in-side. When she came back, she was carrying one with lots of gold and red and green. She unfolded it. "Here," she said, handing it to Mother, "you can have this one. The stitches," she explained without apologizing, "are a little big. I stitched this one the year that I had cataracts."

Mother, who was pleased to have the quilt, was also interested in hearing more about the cataracts. Her father, my other grandfather, had been a physician. She has al-ways encouraged me in my plans to follow in his footsteps.

"Do you still have them?" she asked.

Aunt Reesa said no. She had gone to her doctor when they got too bad and he had put her in his chair, set an eggcup on her eye, and sucked them out. She didn't even need a bandage afterward. Just take it easy for a few days, he told her, and fitted her with reading glasses.

When we got home, Mother borrowed a book on cata-racts from the library. "'Couching,'" she read to Perley and me, "'was practiced by the ancients. It consisted of dislocating the lens downward and backward into the vitreous chamber. The first mention of couching appears in records of Celsus, a Roman physician of the first century A.D. It persisted until the early eighteenth century.'" Mother looked up. "For all we know," she said, "it still persists in Carolina." She continued reading. "'In addition to two modern forms of surgery, there is a relatively new procedure known as phacoemulsification. Using an ultrasonic needle to suck out the cataract, it allows the patient to return to all activities immediately afterward.'" The book warned, however, that this last was a technique requiring utmost practice and proficiency and was therefore rarely done. "Rarely done where?" Mother wondered aloud. "Perhaps in Carolina it is an everyday event."

On the way home from Uncle Ben's farm, Perley startled all of us by asking Daddy, "How did you kill the mule?" Daddy understandably looked puzzled.

"On the farm," said Perley. "How did you kill the mule when you were a boy on your grandfather's farm?"

"He means," I explained, understanding dawning, "did you shoot him or what?"

"The mule pulled the plow," Daddy replied. He sounded genuinely shocked. "Why would we have killed him?"

"When he got too old." Perley insisted, never one to give up easily. "When he got too old to pull the plow, how did you kill him then?"

"We never did," said Father. "As I recall, when he got old, we turned him out to graze. His name was Hank," he added, as though to clinch it. "Besides, what would a person do with a dead mule anyway?"

*   *   *

Now it happens that in my life I have read more than a few books. When I was Perley's age, in fact, I read every fairy tale that I could lay my hands on. I knew how many stories there were about mules, about muleskins, to be exact. There seemed to be no end to the number of tales in which a farmer or field hand or slave walked through the town, calling out, "Muleskin, muleskin for sale, what will you give for this muleskin for sale?" The muleskin, as I recalled it, had often been the point of the story. I did not share this news with Perley who seems to find no shortage of concerns without my help. It did, however, cross my mind for the first time that minute that a person such as Perley who spent so much time reading the encyclopedia would naturally miss out on some important information. I did mention it, though, to Father later.

"Where do you suppose," I asked him, "they got so many muleskins from in the first place?"

Father looked at me and wrinkled his forehead. Then he pushed my hair back off my face as he used to do when I was little.

"Sometimes," he said slowly, "a mule will die of old age. Did you ever think of that?" Actually I hadn't. I would think about it later, but right then I thought instead of moose and about another nature show I'd watched with Perley on educational television.

The show was about moose being driven from their land by people who wanted it for other purposes. Every year there was less land and less food for the moose. It was wintertime; the cameraman had focused in on a single moose that was dying. The moose was aged and majestic; his antlers were enormous. Coyotes prowled in the background waiting. Soon, said the narrator, the moose would be too weak to fight them off. He looked too weak already, but the coyotes, knowing better, kept their distance. The camera lens zoomed in as the moose pawed at the ground, circled, and lay down. "This will be his final resting place," said the narrator. "He will not get up again." The coyotes crept closer. Just as I thought I could not bear to watch another minute, the narrator's voice took on added resonance as he described the next scene, which viewers could plainly see. "Three grown moose from out of the hills," he intoned, "have come to take up a deathwatch beside their old friend, or rival. They are paying their last respects to a fallen comrade." There they stayed by his side, until his final breath was taken. Only then, when he was dead, did the other three move on.

"My glasses are foggy," Perley had complained, wriggling along the sofa until his body touched mine.

"So are my eyes," I told him, and tried to smile as I wiped them.

"Was your mule's name really Hank?" I asked Daddy.

"It was." He nodded. "He even had an old straw hat he wore with holes for his ears to stick through, and on his hat my grandmother had embroidered his name. Believe me," he said, "that was one mule who died of old age."

I believed him then, and I still believe him now. It seems to me I don't have that much choice.

3 🐌
Aunt Sister's House

SISTER is what nearly everyone who knows her calls Daddy's oldest sister. "Get sister to help you do this. Get sister to help you do that," their mother was forever telling Daddy when both of them were children until it finally became her name. Her real name though is Henry George, which she has always tried to keep to herself. Almost the only ones who know it anymore are relatives, and some of them have forgotten.

"You can call me Georgia," she tells people when she meets them for the first time.

"Georgia is an interesting name," Mother said before she knew.

"Ummm," said Daddy. "If I were you," he suggested, "I wouldn't mention it to Sister."

"Why is that?" asked Mother.

"She's sensitive about her name."

"You mean on account of being named for a state?"

"Georgia," Father explained, "is not her first name."

"What is her first name?" Mother persisted.

"Henry," he said. "She was named for Mother's oldest brother."

"I can see," Mother said, "why she'd prefer using her middle name."

"Georgia is not her middle name either," Father continued.

What is her middle name? would have been Mother's next question, but she didn't have to ask it.

"Her name is Henry George," he said with a tone of finality. "She was named after both of Mother's brothers."

"Maybe they were hoping for a boy," I said. It didn't surprise me when no one answered. I did realize, of course, I wasn't the one to criticize.

"Named after an uncle, were you?" a school bus driver once asked me.

"Cyd*ra*," I told him, "with a *C*."

"Oh," he said then, entirely uninterested.

My mother, whose name is Alexis, is one of the few people I know who like their names. "I was always glad," she once said, "that I was born first and didn't get stuck with such a plain name as Alice."

The day after Granddad's funeral Mother, Daddy, Perley, and I spend at Aunt Sister's. Grandmother prefers staying home with only Ms. Lewis to help her. Ms. Lewis has worked now and then for Grandmother for years.

Aunt Sister's house is unusually large, even in this family. It contains six bedrooms, each having its own private bathroom, a large living room with three steps leading down into it, and an adjacent but entirely separate dining room. There also are a television room, a paneled den, a sitting room, so called for lack of any better name, a finished basement with a Ping-Pong table in it, and a kitchen that features an open-pit barbecue at its center; plus it has a skylight. There is a tennis court in the backyard, but no swimming pool.

"I can swim at the college," says Aunt Sister, who is a professor of cultural anthropology. Well, I'm sure she could play tennis there, too, but I've never heard her mention it. Her husband, Uncle Phillip, is a neurologist on the teaching staff of the university. When we visit them, Mother and I are in our element examining the bookshelves. Mother compares medical texts with her home cures, and I hope for a head start in premed school.

They have three children, all of whom naturally came home for the funeral. Cousin Tineen is a first-year prelaw student at the University of Virginia; her brother, P.C., is an engineer who lives in Boston; and Mattie, the eldest, is a schoolteacher. She plans to get married next year.

The most interesting thing about their house, besides its sheer size, is the appliances. There are hidden buttons in most of the rooms, which when pressed cause doors to open and close, shelves to raise and lower, objects such as stereos to take themselves out and put themselves away. Nor is that all. There is one bed that gives massages, another with a water mattress, and a third that goes up and down as in a hospital. In almost all the rooms are television sets, several now connected to computers. An intercom system provides instant communication throughout the house. They were the first family I knew to get a cordless telephone. Mother has difficulty operating it.

"There's nothing to operate," I have tried explaining to her, but she still gets flustered when it rings and if she answers is likely to disconnect the caller. It helps to put Mother's reaction in perspective to know that at home among the things we do not own are a color television, a calculator or computer, a clothes washer much less a dryer, a dishwasher; and certainly we have no cordless telephone. Ours is black with a rotary dial. We also have no air-conditioning, not even a window fan.

"Tell me again," I overheard Father ask one sticky night last summer, "why we don't like air-conditioning."

"It isn't natural," Mother replied. "Besides, wouldn't you rather have a breeze?"

I certainly would have rather had a breeze that night than what we had, over ninety degrees at midnight and not a breath of air stirring. I recalled in seventh grade my home economics teacher asking, "What kitchen appliance does every family have?"

"An iron," I answered. Of course, everyone laughed. "Right," I said, too late, seeing my mistake. "A toaster, I meant." "Blender" turned out to be the correct response. I was glad it wasn't an IQ test.

Mother, of course, doesn't need a blender for the kind of cooking that she does. *The Medieval Honey Book* provides some of her favorite recipes. She is delighted when we have new friends stay for dinner who haven't learned yet that discretion is better than tasting. I myself stay out of the kitchen as much as possible. If I haven't eaten something yet, I see no reason to try it now, is my motto. Perley will try almost anything, including cooking. He can already make bread from scratch. Well, Mother has to light the oven for him. I have friends who look at me in disbelief, hearing that.

"You have an oven you have to light?" they ask.

I shrug. I'm not sure that Mother even knows there is a choice between automatic pilot and electric. Concerning Aunt Sister's house, she has told her own sister, Alice, in wonderment, "It contains articles whose possibilities I've never even considered."

On the occasion of this current visit there is something new to see in the house which isn't electric.

"Did you see the pictures?" Cousin Tineen asks, leading me into the large sitting room, which I suppose might once have been called a parlor. It turns out she is referring to a group of recently hung photographs of ancestors. These do not seem at all the same as the snapshots that covered the walls in Aunt Reesa's home showing relatives past and present, all of whom seemed still intimately connected with the family. Aunt Sister's are formal portraits of posed subjects, elegantly framed and artistically displayed.

"Where did you get them?" Daddy asks as he and his sister join us.

"They were in Mother's attic, just getting ruined. She told me to take whatever I wanted." Aunt Sister lowers her voice. "Now that I've had them restored," she confides to Daddy, "naturally Selena wants some, too."

"Notice Mother's defensive manner," Tineen says later. "It's because she took them all." Tineen, I can see, is already practicing to practice law.

Aunt Sister indicates the nearest picture. "That's of Granddad," she says, meaning the granddad whose farm they spent their summers on.

"I believe it's the first photograph I've ever seen of him," says Daddy. He studies it carefully. I study it carefully, too, seeking clues to both my father and his family in it.

The photograph is black-and-white. It shows a man who may be as old as eighty or as young as sixty. I am not good at judging ages. He is broad-shouldered, but otherwise slender. He holds himself very erect, though most likely he is seated. He has on a three-piece suit, dark in the picture, that looks as if it were constructed of very substantial material. There is a single dark button on the jacket and another showing on the vest and a pin of some sort attached to the lapel. Is it the emblem of an organization to which he belonged or just an ornament? There is no way to tell. His shirt is white, and both the collar and the tie are widely old-fashioned. His hair is white and close-cut, but even so, one can see how tightly it curls. Furrows line his high, wide forehead, and his sparse eyebrows, like Daddy's, seem to arch in surprise. Like Daddy's, his eyes are long across, but narrow, almost Oriental-looking, with an extra fold that slants downward, lending them a hooded and slightly mysterious air. His cheekbones are pronounced. His nose and mouth are broad. His lips look chiseled, as if put there by a sculptor. His expression is solemn, no doubt befitting such a serious occasion as sitting for a portrait photograph.

I try to recall what little I know about the man in the picture. A person couldn't tell from the photograph that he was a farmer or know his hands had even ever touched the soil. I remember that last year in school there was an exhibit of photographs from the Smithsonian taken in the 1930s as part of the federal Works Progress Administration. Among them were several of black farmers in Mississippi and in Alabama. One man in each group stood out. He was explaining to the others how to raise their crops. The men explaining were cooperative extension agents. I ask my father now whether his granddad was such an agent. He says that he doesn't know but that it's possible. I look at the picture some more. He looks like a man whom other men would listen to.

Daddy squeezes my elbow, and we move to the opposite side of the room, where there is a picture of a woman who looks about the same age that Grandmother is now. She is wearing glasses. Her hair is stylishly smooth, just covering her ears. Her skin is even-toned. Her dress, a flowered print, hangs loosely from her shoulders. There is a string of beads around her neck. Though her ears are covered by her hair, the hoops she wears in them can just be seen. She holds her head exceedingly straight, and except that she is heavier than is presently fashionable, even now she would be considered very beautiful.

"Do you know who she is?" Aunt Sister asks.

Of course, we don't.

"That's Mother's aunt Helen," she informs us.

I met her once a long time ago. We had gone to see her in a hospital. I thought then that I had never seen anyone so ancient or so small. She could hardly speak. She had reached out a hand and touched me.

"I remember her," I say.

Aunt Sister opens a credenza drawer and pokes around in it. She extracts a piece of wrinkled paper which turns out to be her great-aunt Helen's funeral program and reads it:

> Helen Puryear Hamilton was born and raised in Alabama. She attended a two-year college there, after which she worked as an extension agent, teaching women canning, nutrition, and how to raise their children. When she was forty-five, she married Charles Hamilton. They had three daughters. When the youngest started school, she returned to college at Howard University in Washington, D.C., and earned her teaching degree. She taught school for twenty years.

"It's a hard story to believe, isn't it?" Aunt Sister asks. "Well, she was over one hundred when she died."

I find true stories are often hard to believe. I remember when I first heard a black woman had created Coca-Cola. I was surprised not just to hear it but, having heard it, to think I had never heard it before.

"Oh, but she did," Alice Walker, the writer, had said on public television. Ms. Walker, on a class trip, had seen a statue of what appeared to be a black woman in the foyer of the Coca-Cola mansion outside Atlanta. Nobody she asked could tell her who the woman was or why she was there. Alice Walker began to doubt what she saw. Then at her own high school graduation the commencement speaker, a horticulturist from Atlanta, had confirmed that it was so. The statue, he said, was of the black woman who had invented Coca-Cola.

There are other pictures in the room. One is of Daddy's grandmother, a tiny woman with thick, wavy hair parted in the middle and pulled back, probably into a coil behind her head. She looks a lot like pictures I have seen of American Indians. She is wearing a full-length white dress with a square collar that shows off her long, graceful neck. Her hands rest folded in her lap, and her legs are crossed at the knees. She isn't smiling, but her expression is serene.

"She is the one I once bit a man for," Daddy says.

"You did what?" I ask.

"There was a man who came to the farm," he explains, "angry about something. He raised his voice to my grandmother, and I rushed after him and bit him on his leg."

A smaller picture beside that one has three people in it. A man is seated, and a woman, no doubt his wife, stands behind him, her hand resting on his shoulder. A baby is cradled in his lap. Both parents are smiling, but the baby stares solemnly out at the viewer. There is a white ribbon in her hair. Aunt Sister says the baby is Melanie, one of Daddy's fourth or fifth cousins, but you would never know it from the picture. The cousin, who lives near Grandmother, is very tall and very stout and laughs all the time.

It is hard to imagine this serious child growing up to be Melanie.

One more photograph, in Sepia, shows a balding, heavy-set man, Grandmother's father. He has on glasses, the familiar white shirt and tie. Pens are sticking out of his pocket; one hand is on his hip; the other rests on something out of the picture, perhaps the framework of the opened door. His mouth is turned down slightly, and I see in surprise my father's mouth, which sometimes turns down that same way. The man's stern expression is indecipherable. Is it anger on his face, or just determination? Is he watching something going on outside or glaring at the photographer whose camera has invaded his privacy? Did the flash of the bulb take him by surprise? His is the only unposed photograph in the room.

"What was he like?" I ask.

But Daddy doesn't know. "He died before I was born," he answers.

The last photograph Aunt Sister shows us hasn't been hung yet. It's of my father. It is strange, but I have never seen a picture of him before as a child. I have seen snapshots taken of him in college. They show a skinny young man, studious, with a worried smile and a constant slouch, who bears little resemblance to the way I think of him. Aunt Sister's photograph seems a better likeness.

The child in it looks about eleven. He is dressed up for the occasion in a suit, starched shirt, and tie. There are two buttons on each sleeve, and his shirt cuffs are fashionably showing. A handkerchief is peeking from his pocket. His hair is so short his head almost looks shaved. What catches one's attention, though, is his expression. There is no hint of a smile anywhere on his face. My lips are sealed, he seems to be saying. His arms are crossed, his elbows firmly planted on what must have been a tabletop. His eyes stare directly out from the picture. It would be impossible even to guess at what this little boy might be thinking.

I search the face for reminders of Perley. The ears, I think, noticing for the first time that both of them have pointy ears. There is not that much resemblance, I decide, then realize it is not a similarity of features that marks them as relatives, but the expression of purposefulness on both their faces.

Later I ask Mother why we don't hang photographs on our walls. "Why do we keep ours in closets?"

Someday, she says, she plans to put them in a scrapbook or have them framed for display. When we return home, she does go so far as to take boxes of pictures out of her closet and examine them. Then she puts them all back.

"There is something in me," she says, "that doesn't love a photograph."

I wonder if it's because she is an artist who paints for a living. Then I remember when her own father was dying, she had taken his photograph from a shelf in my grandmother's closet and set it on the dresser in the room where he lay. He was wearing his doctor clothes in it. It almost seemed to me at the time she was trying to remind him who he was. After he died, she had a copy of the photo made for herself. She stores it in a trunk with her important papers. "I'm afraid," she said when she put it there, "looking at it will make me remember him wrong."

4

Perley

WHEN Perley was born, I raised the question of his name. "I can't believe you'd really do that to him!" I considered eight years of coping with "Cydra" had made me an expert on names.

"Do what to him?" Mother asked calmly. "What is she talking about?" she inquired of Father.

"It's so old-fashioned," I explained. "Everyone will tease him."

"It's Daddy's name, and Granddad's," Mother pointed out. "No one teases them."

"Sure," I said, "but you don't hear them use it either," and that is the truth. Perley Robert Williams is their name, with a "Jr." added onto Daddy's. Granddad was mostly called Will, sometimes William, and Daddy goes by the name of Rob.

"Maybe your brother will have a nickname, too," said Mother. But he never did.

He was Perley from the start, and even I would have to agree it seems to suit him. Also, he likes it.

When he was four, he came home from his first day of nursery school, elated, to announce, "Guess what! There are three Jims in my class, two Barbaras, one Suzy, one Susan, and one Suzine, who comes from Korea." He paused to take a breath. "I'm the only Perley.

"Guess what!" he said again. "My teacher said I have an interesting name." He could hardly stop talking about it. Finally he looked at me.

"If you were in my class," he said kindly, "you'd be the only Cyd. The only *girl* Cyd," he amended. "You have an interesting name for a girl." Perley has always been mature about not hurting other people's feelings.

Perley has always been mature period. He could read even before he started regular school.

"What are you reading, Perley?" Granddad asked when Perley was five and we were visiting. Perley had a newspaper propped in front of him at the kitchen table, imitating our mother, I assumed.

"About crickets," Perley replied enthusiastically. "Did you know a cricket's ear is in its front leg? It hears with its elbow." Granddad leaned over to see what Perley was reading.

"Amazing," he said.

I, concentrating on the cricket's ear, missed the point. At that stage in my life I was given to considering ways of improving the human species. If, for instance, the mouth had been located on the stomach, swallowing would be unnecessary. I had not previously contemplated relocating the ear, however, so Perley's information was of interest. This line of reasoning was interrupted by Granddad's asking, "Isn't anybody listening? I'm telling you, Perley can read." That was how we found out.

It wasn't long after that when Perley got his first pair of glasses. "Can you read better now?" I asked.

"Not better, Cydra," he said in his serious way, "just faster."

"I wonder why he never told us," Mother said.

"Probably," suggested Granddad, "since everyone around him does it all the time, he thought it was a skill like walking, not worth mentioning."

I looked at Granddad quickly to see if he meant something in particular by this, but if he did, I couldn't tell. Walking could be a sore point with Perley, who sometimes did it in his sleep.

Once he walked right out the door of the apartment where we lived, took the elevator up, and rang the doorbell of the man who lived above us. True apartment dwellers that we were, we didn't know the man, although occasionally we passed him in the lobby. When he answered his bell and saw Perley there, so far as we ever discovered, he only said, "You must have the wrong apartment, sonny," then closed his door. Perley found his way back home, awake and shaking. He was afraid to go to sleep at night for weeks afterward.

"Perley," I suggested, "if you sleep with your key around your neck, you'll always be able to get back in." Mother wasn't pleased, to put it mildly.

"He could hang himself." She exaggerated, meaning he could choke on the chain.

The only reason Perley had a key to begin with was that I had one, and in those days whatever I had he wanted. He certainly didn't need one. Mother, who had never gone back to work in an office after he'd been born, was usually home at her drawing board, or when she was out, Perley was with her. It was a great advantage to his coming. I liked having her at home when I got back from school.

"You can have a key," she finally told him, "only if you promise not to take it out of the apartment." She didn't want him to lose it. Perley readily agreed, logic not being a four-year-old's strong point.

Mother did begin propping a chair against the hallway door before she went to sleep at night. She also looked up somnambulism in a reference book in the library. There is no specific cause, she learned, nor any known cure. The condition is often outgrown. Also, according to the book, in an otherwise normal person there seem to be no ill effects, not counting, of course, if one falls down a stairway or encounters some other similar disaster while doing it. Mother and Daddy both seemed relieved.

"Well, sure," I said, "but are we certain Perley is an otherwise normal person?" I, for one, was not *that* positive.

"Perley," I asked him one day when he was still in kindergarten, "what are you drawing?"

"A person," he replied.

"A man person or a woman person?"

"I don't know," he answered in the earnest manner he still has. "I'm not up to that part yet."

"I see," I said, peering more closely at his drawing.

It was at about that same time Perley started putting bathrooms in the houses that he drew. Once he drew a police station and put in a men's room and a ladies' room. Mother was called into school for a parent-teacher conference.

"Do you think something may be troubling him?" the teacher asked.

"Oh no," Mother airily explained. "I'm an artist myself. Probably," she confided, "he gets his sense of realism from me."

The teacher cleared her throat. "Perhaps," she said, "he has some unresolved conflict over his family situation."

It took several minutes for it to dawn on Mother what the teacher meant. "What do you mean?" she asked the teacher.

The teacher mumbled something that included "interracial," which was definitely a mistake. Mother does not care even to hear that word. "It always sounds to me like a sociological experiment," she says.

"Tell me," Mother asked, "exactly what is it about bathrooms that you find objectionable? I myself," she said, "find them a convenience. We have two at home. I wouldn't consider an apartment without one." Standing, she brought the conference to a close.

"I guess I told her," she told Daddy at home that evening while I eavesdropped. All she said to Perley, though, was: "Your teacher doesn't care for bathrooms in drawings. Please do her a favor and leave them out. You can fill them in when you get home."

"It sounds like good advice for getting ahead," I told him.

Perley concurred. "Not just in regular school either. It's good advice even for Sunday school."

"Why?" I asked. "Have you been drawing bathrooms in your Bible stories?"

"Don't be silly, Cydra," he said, and went on to explain. "There are things you can't take as gospel, even in Sunday school. You need some salt."

"As in grain of salt?"

He nodded. "Take the whale, for instance," he said. "Jonah got swallowed by the whale, right?"

"Right." I agreed.

"Wrong," said Perley. "Jonah was swallowed by a fish, a big fish. The Bible *says* fish, in the first place. In the second place, there are no whales and have never been in the Mediterranean, which was where Jonah went swimming. And in the third place," he said conclusively, "a whale's throat is too small to swallow a man."

"I see," I said.

"You know the story about Adam, Eve, the apple, and the snake?" he continued. I nodded. "Well, there probably was no apple," he informed me. "The Bible says only that Eve gave Adam some fruit. It doesn't say what kind. It could have been a pear or even a fig from the same tree that the fig leaves came. Also," he went on with barely a pause, "the pictures showing Eve about to eat the apple and the snake are wrong. The snake," he pointed out with perfect logic, "did not become a snake until Eve ate the fruit and God found out about it. Until then," Perley finished, "the snake had two legs and stood straight up the same as people."

"Have you discussed this with the other children?" I asked him, curious.

"That is what I'm trying to tell you, Cyd," he said. "Sometimes to do well, and not just in school, a person has to do less than he knows." Perley was always a fast learner.

His story reminded me of one I knew about a snake. I used to accompany Mother to storytelling festivals which she attended, hoping to find folktales to illustrate and sell. While she occasionally did, but usually didn't, I acquired a repertoire of stories I still know.

"Do you want to hear my snake story?" I asked Perley. "Is it from the Bible?"

"Not exactly," I said. "It's African, from Ghana." I told it to him as I'd heard it.

We do not mean, that is, we do not really mean what we are about to say is so. You see Snake the way he is now; he has no legs. But he was not always that way. In the beginning all the animals had legs, even Snake, and they all lived together peaceably tilling the soil. Each animal had a job to do. Elephant pulled down the trees and cleared the trunks away. Deer chopped up the soil, and Fennec made the holes. Birds flew low and dropped seeds into them, which Hedgehog covered over.

Everyone had work except for Snake. Snake was *so* lazy. Whenever there was something he *could* do, he had an excuse for why he couldn't. Maybe it was a sick grandmother he had to go and look after, or a sister's wedding, but anyway, he never helped.

When it came time to harvest the crops and the animals went to the fields, they discovered that someone had been stealing their best vegetables. They were very angry. They called a meeting and invited all the animals to come. We must catch that thief, they said, but how? They asked Anansi, that very clever spider, so good with problem solving. Anansi said he would go home and think it over and come up with a plan. While he was thinking, though, he wanted the animals to promise that they would not go near the fields. Naturally they promised.

But that night Anansi did not go home as he had said. No, he didn't. Instead, he got his two sons, Kwaku and Kuma, and they got a bucket of tar and spread it all over the vegetable field. Then Anansi climbed to the top of a tall tree and waited. He waited and waited, and sometime about midnight he heard a moaning and a groaning, and a voice called, "Help me. I'm stuck in the tar. Please won't somebody help me?" But Anansi stayed right where he was high in that tree. When morning came, he climbed down and gathered the other animals. Together they returned to the field. There, stuck in the tar, they found that lazy Snake. Were those animals ever angry. They picked up sticks and stones to beat Snake with, but Anansi told them no. Kind as well as wise, he said that they should let Snake go. Of course, that was more easily said than done. When the animals tried to pull Snake from that field, he did not budge. Overnight, you see, the tar had hardened, and he was stuck fast in it. Then the animals got a long, strong rope, and they wrapped it all around Snake, and they pulled and they pulled. Snake stretched and stretched, and then, suddenly, he came loose. But his legs did not come loose. There they stayed fast in that tar. Then the animals felt bad for what they had done, so they rubbed Snake's wounds with clay and bound them in leaves and took him home. They waited and waited, and after some time his wounds had all healed, but his legs never grew back again, and to this day Snake is very long and very stretchy.

Perley liked the story. I guess to pay me back for it, the next time he came home from Sunday school he told me a story he had heard. A woman had told it to his class that morning about her grandson Billy.

When Billy had been eight, his grandmother had to leave him for an hour by himself. "Just stay in the yard," she told him. She meant the front yard. "Son, don't you go out that gate" were her very last words to him as she was leaving, just before she kissed him goodbye. Of course, Billy promised he wouldn't. Now, the minute that he said it he truly meant it, but it wasn't too long after his grandmother was gone that Billy ran out of interesting things to do. He had picked flowers and dug in the dirt.

He was tired of looking at his book. He thought if he just took a few steps out of that yard, nothing bad would come of it and his grandmother would never know. He planned to come right back. So he took a few steps, then a few more, and the next thing Billy knew he was next door on the neighbor's front lawn, and he wasn't alone. The neighbors were gone, but there was a very large dog in the yard. Whether it was a biting dog or not, of course, he couldn't be sure.

Biting was the reason the lady in Sunday school had said that parents and grandparents were forever warning children against petting dogs they didn't know unless the dogs were with their owners and the children asked permission first.

Billy may not have listened to his grandmother about staying in the yard, but he did have enough sense to know she was right about strange dogs. Therefore, he did the only thing that he could think to do: He climbed the large tree that stood in the middle of that lawn. He climbed it all the way to the top, which was very high. The dog did not climb the tree. Dogs, as everybody knows, are not very good climbers. That is the reason cats are forever getting away from them. The dog didn't climb the tree, but neither did he go away. He stayed right there at the bottom, looking up. Billy knew that if he did not get down from that tree soon, his grandmother would come home and find out he had left the yard and he would be in a lot of trouble. Just at that minute he saw three children whom he had never seen before, even though he had lived on that block all of his life. He called out to them for help. The children, strangers, mind you, to Billy, came to his aid. They picked up stones and threw them at the dog. The dog ran away. Billy climbed down from the tree, thanked the children, and went home, closing the gate behind him. Afterward he always obeyed his grandmother.

"You heard that story in Sunday school?" I asked Perley, truly astounded. Perley nodded, pleased to have remembered it. "About throwing stones at a dog and deceiving a grandmother?"

"Oh," Perley said, "I forgot. The story had a moral."

"I should hope so," I said.

"The moral was that Jesus must have sent those three children to help Billy get home."

After Perley went away, I thought about it. I considered the possibility that being only five, he had left out some parts or remembered them wrong. I couldn't understand why anyone, much less Jesus, would send three children to help Billy when he was disobeying. Wouldn't God have wanted Billy's grandmother to find out? Also, why would a Sunday school story include children throwing stones at a dog that hadn't even done anything wrong? No one had told the dog to stay in its own yard after all. I called Perley back.

"That was a really good story," I told him.

"Thank you," he said modestly.

"However," I said, "as you know, I have read some stories in my time." Perley nodded. "Therefore, I know there is always more than one way to end any tale. For instance," I explained, "in 'Cinderella,' sometimes the two wicked sisters get to live happily ever after and sometimes they have their eyes pecked out by birds. And in 'Rapunzel, Rapunzel, let down your hair,' sometimes Rapunzel winds up with twin children at the end and sometimes she doesn't." I could have gone on, but I saw I had his attention. "The point is," I said, "it seems to me there might be a happier ending to your story." Perley found it hard to conceive of any ending happier than Billy's getting home before his grandmother and his grandmother's never finding out, but he was willing to listen.

"Okay," I said. "Consider Billy at the top of that tree as he looked down. Number one, he was afraid he would fall. Number two, he was afraid his grandmother would come home and find him gone. And number three, it looked like rain, and he was afraid either he would get drenched or the branch he was on would blow down in the storm, in which case he would both get drenched and fall and his grandmother would be sure to hear about it.

"He called down to that dog. 'Dog,' he called, 'are you a biting dog?' Naturally the dog didn't answer, so he tried again. 'Dog,' he called a little louder, 'are you a biting dog or not?' The dog still didn't answer. He tried a third time. 'Dog,' he called in his loudest voice, 'if you are not a biting dog, then wag your tail.' Well, that dog was so pleased finally to get someone's attention, even only a little boy's in a tree, he wagged his tail and made happy little noises in his throat. Billy edged down the tree just a little. He broke off a twig. 'Dog,' he said, 'I'll throw this stick, and if you are not a biting dog, you fetch it.' Billy threw the stick, and the dog chased it. Now you might think that with the dog chasing that stick Billy could have climbed down and run home, but he was a little higher in the tree than he had thought. The dog came back with the stick, lay down beside the tree, and looked up. Billy broke off a second twig and threw it just a little farther. This time, when the dog brought it back, he had begun to look a tiny bit tired. Billy threw a third stick. The dog fetched that one, too, but when he returned with it, he was panting.

"Billy, in the meantime, had gotten himself as close to the bottom of the tree as he could by climbing down the branches. All there was now between him and the ground was tree trunk, and it looked a lot farther down from where he sat than it had when he'd been down there looking up.

"'Okay, dog,' said Billy, 'just stay there where you are.' The dog didn't budge. It just lay there, panting by the tree. Billy closed his eyes. He spread his arms and said a little prayer; then he jumped. Exactly as he had planned, he landed on that dog, who wasn't hurt a bit and turned out definitely not to be a biting dog.

"The upshot was, Billy took the dog home with him, and when his grandmother got back, he told her what he'd done and how the dog had saved his life. 'That tree is very high,' he said. 'A storm was coming up. It was windy. The dog stretched out beneath the branch on which I sat, and something came over me and told me—jump.' If that dog had not been there, Billy assured his grandmother, he might have broken his neck and died in the fall. At the very least, he said, he would have broken an arm or a leg. 'Can we keep the dog?' he begged."

"Could he?" asked Perley.

"Probably," I said. "Yes, I'm sure of it. Billy's grandmother was so pleased he had told the truth and learned his lesson that she said they would put up signs advertising for the owner. If no one came to claim the dog, she said, Billy could keep it. And that's what happened. Billy named the dog Tree."

"Tree," said Perley, "is a funny name for a dog."

"Well," I said, "its real name was Tremont, but Billy always called him Tree for short."

5

I, Cydra

PICTURE a picture, a moving picture: I, Cydra, age eight, coming home, running home from school, so happy that day and in so much of a hurry. Perley wasn't born yet, though Mother was already pregnant with him. She still worked in the art department of an advertising agency, and Daddy did what he did: made deals; earned money; took business trips.

"What does your father do?" children I went to school with asked.

"Do when?" I'd ask them back, stalling, hoping they'd forget their question.

"For a living. What does he do for a living?"

"A spy," I said once. "I think he's a spy." I was joking.

"It's not a funny joke," said Mother. "Why can't you just tell them he's in real estate?"

"Is he?" I asked.

"He buys and sells. It depends what there's a market for. There's usually a market for land," she said in her exasperated voice.

"My father's a salesman," I told the other children.

"Where?" they wanted to know.

"Downtown," I answered vaguely.

"Oh," they said then, too bored to pursue it.

That particular day, which I remember was a Thursday, I let myself into the apartment, locked the door behind me as I was supposed to do, and went straight to my bedroom. I didn't even bother with milk and the cookies Mother left me every school day in a fancy dish in the kitchen. I was in too much of a hurry. I took a shower and washed my hair. I would have preferred a bath with Mother's bath salts but didn't want to take the chance I might not be ready on time. I dried my hair, then sprayed Mother's perfume behind my ears and into the crooks of my elbows and knees. I put on my best blue dress over a new satiny slip, my only pair of white lace tights, and my just-bought shiny black patent leather shoes. I got the only pocketbook I owned out from my closet.

I examined myself in Mother's full-length mirror. I saw a girl, medium tall for her age and on the slim side, with sandy-colored hair parted exactly in the middle and pulled back into a ponytail. She was pale, with freckles on her nose and under her eyes. Her eyes were wide-set, brown flecked with green. She had a small mouth, a pointed chin, and a long neck.

I rubbed a tiny bit of Mother's lightest lipstick on my

fingertip and then transferred the color to my mouth. There, I thought, it's the best that I can do. I went into the front foyer, sat down on the chair beside the little table near the door, and waited. I rested my patent leather shoes on the wooden chair rung as I was not supposed to do. I was too excited even to try reading a book.

The reason for the state that I was in, my clothes and my excitement, was that in just a few minutes my REAL FATHER was coming to take me out to dinner. "I'm going out to dinner tonight with my REAL FATHER," I had told the children in school. That I had not seen him since I was a baby only made it seem that much more romantic.

"Wow," Caroline Silvers had said during social studies when I told her. "Doesn't it just make you dizzy? Imagine, a date with your own father." Caroline was without doubt the most sophisticated child in third grade.

What misgivings I had, I'd managed with a surprising degree of success to push to the back of my mind. I dismissed a vague feeling of disloyalty concerning Daddy, who was actually my stepfather but had always treated me as his. My REAL FATHER, whom I thought about in capital letters to distinguish him from Daddy, was a total stranger to me and had never shown the slightest interest in altering that condition. He was coming to see me now only as a result of my persistence.

At age eight I had an immoderate bent for drama. I had pestered Mother unceasingly until she'd finally undertaken the troublesome task of locating the man to whom she'd been so briefly married and whose biological child I was.

"Why must you look for trouble?" she had said by way of trying to dissuade me.

"He *is* my REAL FATHER," I had replied self-righteously.

"I see" was all Mother said.

"I'm a traveling man," he told me by way of explanation when I finally caught up with him by telephone.

"Well, sure," I said, hoping I sounded like an understanding grown-up, "but sometimes you surely must travel to New York."

"Sometimes." There was a longish pause. "I'll tell you what," he said, "next time I do, I'll look you up. We'll go to dinner. Would you like that?"

I thought it would be heaven. "That would be lovely," I answered in my Caroline Silvers voice. Mother looked at me sidewise from where she stood.

Picture a picture one more time, a still frame, a photograph that does not move: I, Cydra, all dressed up in my best clothes, sitting on the chair in the foyer, one foot in its patent leather shoe tucked under me, the other wrapped around a chair leg, clutching in my lap the only pocketbook I own. Outside, it is starting to get dark. Inside, I wait and make excuses for someone else's lateness.

That was when the telephone rang.

"Hey, Cydra," boomed the voice of my REAL FATHER.

"Hi," I said back, trying to match his heartiness, "I bet you're running late." It was an attempt to forestall the inevitable. "Running late" was what Daddy often told me when he called: "Running late, baby, meet me in the lobby," or "Running late, sugar, grab the shirts in the hall. We'll drop them off at the cleaner's on the way to your school."

This person on the telephone wasn't running late. "I hate to do this to you," said the stranger's voice, "but I'm going to have to break our date." I heard voices in the background. "You understand how it is with business. Look, kid, next time I'm in New York, I'll make it up to you. Hey, I'm calling from a pay phone, be sweet now, I have to run."

I sat there numb for several minutes, holding onto the telephone. After hanging up, I tried to decide what to do. I could change my clothes, have milk and cookies, do my homework. I couldn't seem to get the order right, and when I tried to stand, it seemed I moved in slow motion. I was still sitting there that same way half an hour later, when Daddy got home.

Act natural, I told myself as he bent to kiss me. That was when I started crying. Once started, I couldn't seem to stop. It must have frightened Daddy because even given to melodrama as I was that year, I was very restrained about crying. After seeing how useless his efforts were to find out what was wrong, he concentrated on calming me down. He picked me up, sat himself in the chair, and held me in his lap. He rocked both of us back and forth as he would with a baby. He patted my head. "It's okay," he kept saying. "Everything will be okay."

No person can cry forever, and eventually I stopped. Daddy stood me up, got a dishtowel, wet it, and washed my face in the kitchen. "Don't budge," he said, then got Mother's hairbrush from her dresser and redid my hair. He plaited it into a single braid, which he pinned on top of my head.

"There," he said, looking down at me, "that's better. Now then, what's the problem, Cyd?"

He has posed that question to me since I've known him: What's the problem, Cyd? Usually it has the effect of seeming to reduce my problems to manageable proportions, but not that time.

I tried to tell him. "My father doesn't love me. He doesn't love me at all. He doesn't even care anything about me." I was struck again as I said it by its awful enormity.

"I see," he said, understanding at once which father we were discussing. Before I could start crying again, he swooped me up and sat me on a shelf above the kitchen counter so that I was eye to eye with him.

"Listen to me, Cyd," he said. "This is important. I love you. I love you very much. I will never stop loving you. You can count on that forever."

"Well, sure," I said in my eight-year-old anticlimactic way, not recognizing real drama when finally I was face-to-face with it, "but what about after the new baby comes? Then I'll just be in the way. I mean," I continued, not really sure what I meant, "the baby will be yours completely, yours and Mom's."

"Cydra, look at me," said Daddy. I looked at him. "If someone were to ask me what child I wanted, exact and in every detail, you would be that child."

"Really?"

"Really." Then he lifted me from where I was and set me down. "Would you do me the honor," he asked, "of joining me for dinner?" He left a note for Mom: "Gone to dinner with Cyd. Be back soon. Don't worry. Love, Rob." We had dinner at a diner. The one thing I can't recall about that day was what we ate.

Naturally the next day in school Caroline Silvers wanted to know how my evening had gone. "It was lovely," I told her, and tried to look mysterious. It was the most I ever told her.

Afterward, and for a long time, I thought that was that, that I was over and done with that part of my life. I have since discovered life is never that simple.

"What was Frank like?" I asked my mother a few years ago, Frank being all I've ever called him since that night. "Why did you marry him in the first place?"

"He had his good and bad points," Mother answered, "just as we all do. Life isn't that simple, Cyd," she pointed out.

I have two photographs of him. Once I'd planned to throw them out. "I wouldn't do that, Cyd, if I were you," said Mother. I still sometimes look at them.

In one of them he is wearing a soldier's uniform, short-sleeved and opened at the collar. The picture was taken in Vietnam, and he mailed it home to us. I guess another soldier took it.

The man in the photograph is sitting in a mess hall, holding himself very straight and looking directly into the camera lens. He looks tired and hot. His hair is dark, but hardly visible, fading as it does into the too-dark background of the picture. There are lines across his forehead. His skin, surprisingly untanned for the climate, shines from perspiration. His neck is short and thick; his face looks hard. I could imagine him interrogating a prisoner of war. But then I notice his elbows resting on the table-top; his short-fingered hands and arms look too soft for a soldier. "Well, he wasn't really a soldier," said Mother. "He was a stockbroker." "What was a stockbroker doing in the war?" I asked once. "He was drafted," she said.

The second picture is of a chubby boy, smiling, in a Boy Scout uniform. The dark shirt is buttoned at the collar, and his neck seems not merely short but nonexistent. He has a round face with a dimple in his chin. His expression is more than happy; it is that of a child delighted with himself. The photograph was taken in a studio. It is sharp enough that I can read the letters on his pocket: CUB SCOUT, B.S.A.

It's funny, I think; I have only two pictures, and in both of them he is wearing a uniform. I have wondered if there is any connection. "There are always connections," my mother told me once when I asked her. "The question is whether they're the right ones." I study the photographs carefully. I cannot really see too much of one. Perhaps my mother is correct: I concentrate too much on surfaces. On the other hand, in a photograph what else is there to see? (There is always something to see. Whether we see it or not is another matter. Where have I heard that?) "Why did Frank leave?" I used to ask my mother time and again. "Maybe he left," she said the last time, "because he couldn't see staying."

There is one more photograph, but it isn't mine. It belongs to my mother. I saw it when I was going through a box of her things that she had stuffed into the bottom portion of a cabinet that no one uses. In this photograph my father is standing with his arm around a woman. They seem to be on a balcony, perhaps outside a hotel room. A railing is behind them, and below in the distance are trees and a waterfall. My father is wearing civilian clothes, chinos and a sweater, which are too tight for him. He has gained a lot of weight, and his hairline is receding. He is smiling. He looks very happy. The woman is Asian, probably Vietnamese. She is very slim and dressed in Western clothes with high-heeled pumps and a two-piece flowered suit with a skirt that just covers her knees. She is beautiful. Her dark hair is worn on top of her head, and her eyebrows are like wings above her slanted eyes. Her head is resting on his shoulder. She looks serious and very sad. I imagine that he looks so happy because he is in love. Perhaps he is going home and plans to send for her. Maybe she is sad because he's leaving and she does not believe he ever will. I wonder who will be the right one.

I have no idea where or when the photograph was taken. I cannot ask my mother about it, or how she came to have it, or why she keeps it. Why were you snooping? she would want to know. You would not like it if I went around poking in your closets and dresser, asking questions about what I found.

I put the picture back, and I tried to forget it. I have almost forgotten it, except once I went to look for it again and it was gone. The box was there but not the photograph. Had I only imagined I once saw it? Did Mother throw it out? Did she hide it somewhere else, knowing I had found it and would come back for it again? How does my mother know the things she knows? Sometimes I think that she knows everything about me. Other times I think she doesn't know me at all.

Last year in school we had to write an essay. It was supposed to be autobiographical. This was what I wrote:

Once there was a young girl who had a date to go to the prom with a prince. She waited for him all dressed up in her best clothes. She waited and waited. Outside it grew dark. The prince had promised to send flowers, white roses to complement her new blue gown. It was getting very late, and the flowers hadn't arrived. Hours had gone by. Finally she telephoned the florist in the lobby. They had delivered flowers, they said, to apartment 4-C. The girl lived in 4-E. Well, she thought, they'd sent them to the wrong apartment, was all. She went across the hall. The door to 4-C was ajar. There seemed to be a party going on, so much noise and such commotion. The girl pushed open the door and went inside. In the middle of the room there was a casket. It was an opened casket with a woman in it. The woman was very old, and of course, she was dead. Now the girl could see it was a wake that she was at and not a party. The mourners were eating and drinking, laughing and weeping. No one paid her any mind. They probably thought that she was family. She tiptoed to the casket and peered in it. There were flowers all around. Their aroma made her dizzy. Then she saw the roses, white roses just beside the woman's head. My roses, thought the girl, and took them. She took them back with her to her apartment. She put them in a bowl filled with water. Then she sat down and waited some more. Her prince never came. Finally she took off her prom clothes and put on a nightgown. She put the bowl with the roses into the refrigerator and went to bed. Her mother wasn't home. She'd had to work late that night at the office.

The next morning at breakfast the girl's mother said, "There's a bowl of dead roses in the refrigerator. What do you know about them?"

"They're for a class project," said the girl.

"What sort of class might that be?" asked the mother, attentive even if she couldn't always be home.

"Flower pressing," said the girl. "It's an elective."

"I see," said her mother.

But when the girl pressed the flowers, not knowing how to dry them properly, they turned moldy and malodorous and had to be thrown out. She never heard from the prince again, nor did she care. She did hear, and from a reliable source, that he wasn't a real prince after all, only a Cub Scout dressed up in prince clothing, and proms she eventually discovered are less than they're cracked up to be.

I got a C on my essay. "Interesting and well written," the teacher wrote at the top, "but it was supposed to be autobiographical."

Mine deserved an A, but I let it go. I saw no reason to explain. I had done what was assigned. The only part that I'd made up was the part about the roses.

6 Courtship

THOUGH I consider myself a well-adjusted person, sometimes I envy Perley. His origins, less obscure than mine, are easier to explain. Like normal children, he is half the mother, half the father he lives with. They all have the same last name, which isn't mine. My last name is James.

"James is a first name," Perley points out. "This is my sister, C. J. Williams," he says, introducing me to his friends this year.

"What does she mean, obscure?" Mother asks.

"Explain to whom?" asks Father.

Lucy Adams in third grade came home with me from school. "Your brother is black," she informed me, seeing our new baby. "I see," she said when she was introduced to Daddy. "You have a *step*father." She seemed relieved to know it.

"That explains it," she happily explained to children the next day in school.

Although I'm mortified remembering, there were stages in my life when I was embarrassed to have Daddy come to school. It wasn't that I didn't know better. I knew better, but that did not prevent my stomach turning over or keep my head from pounding before an Open School or PTA night or a relay game with parents.

"You have a very nice father, Cydra," some teacher was certain to say the following day, ignoring all the other children's fathers who'd been there the night before. Well, I did realize some children's fathers never came to school, or almost never did. I fervently wished then that mine was one of them.

Daddy, however, believed it was a parent's obligation to demonstrate interest in the educational progress of his children. It was probably a good thing, too, since Mother felt the same way about her going to school as I felt about Daddy's going. Her stomach hurt, and she got headaches.

"It's hard to explain," she sometimes tried to explain to Daddy. "I know it's immature," she'd say in her maturest voice, "but knowing it doesn't help me." I knew exactly how she felt. Of course, sometimes, as when Perley drew the bathrooms in his pictures or Daddy was away on business trips, she couldn't help herself and went. But as often as she could, she sent Daddy instead or at least made him go with her.

"It's only a stage," Mother said unsympathetically, meaning mine and not hers. "You'll outgrow it."

"See," she reminded me not too long ago, "I was right."

But it was my father who was right. "Don't worry, Cyd," he told me sympathetically. "I understand, believe me. All children are embarrassed by their parents sometimes."

"I'm not," said Mother. "I'm not embarrassed by mine."

"Not this minute," Daddy said, "but I recall one time." He meant she was embarrassed by their cool reception to her marriage, second marriage, marriage to Daddy. At the time she couldn't believe it.

"But why?" she had asked, disbelieving. "Only because he is black? That's your only reason?" She found it especially hard to believe since her father was a physician. She remembered stories that he told of the Depression. Patients paid him in chickens. "Mind you," she said, telling the story, "that was in Brooklyn, a borough of New York City." Mother liked to think of him as a humanitarian. "Otherwise," she'd ask, "what was the point?" Her mother's reaction had surprised her even more. Grandmother had been a newspaperwoman.

"Not just a journalist either," Aunt Alice said at the time, as astounded as Mother. "She was a fiery orator. She stood on crowded street corners, public rallies in her time, and preached the brotherhood of men, the sisterhood of women, equal rights for all and humankindness."

"When will she practice them?" asked Mother.

"Don't worry," Aunt Alice told her. "They'll come around. They have to, or else they'll lose face." Aunt Alice had worked at the United Nations and understood the importance of maintaining face.

As it turned out, however, it wasn't loss of face that made them come around. It was Perley.

"What a beautiful baby," Grandmother said, holding him that first time.

Grandpa was already sick by then. Mother put Perley in his lap. "So," he said, "there'll be another doctor in the family."

I regarded him suspiciously. "I'm going to be a doctor," I reminded everyone.

"That's what I said," he said. "You'll be one and Perley will be another one. Didn't you just hear me say that?"

Mother laughed. It reminded me of all the times she called him on the telephone to tell him jokes. "See," she'd say, smiling in satisfaction when he got a punch line, "even sick with all his medicine, his mind is as sharp as a tack." Sometimes it wasn't. Sometimes he couldn't even hear her. Sometimes he heard but couldn't hold onto the phone. Sometimes his throat closed with no warning, and he couldn't answer. Those times Grandmother took the receiver from him and told Mother impatiently that he was too sick to make jokes. Mother only shrugged sadly then, knowing her own mother was worried, not angry.

Now, almost age ten, Perley thinks that I'm the lucky one. "You have all the memories," he says.

"That's just because I'm older," I explain in my older voice.

"It's not just that," he insists. "You were there at the start. Golly, Cydra, you were the one who introduced them." "Golly" was his favorite word for a long time. I was glad when he gave it up in favor of "don't you see," as in "Don't you see, Cyd, if it weren't for you, I wouldn't even be here."

"Tell me again," Perley asks now and then, "what it was like when Mom and Dad met." I'm reminded of myself when I was his age.

"Tell me again, Mom," I used to beg. "What was it like when you and Dad met?"

"Cyd," she'd reply, invariably surprised, "you introduced us." That is the truth so far as it goes; but I was barely five then, and my memories are vague. I have to take Mother's word for most of it. I used to curl up on her bed the way Perley does on mine and make her tell me from the start.

Her telling brought back bits and pieces until at last I'd say, "Yes, that's how it was. It's exactly how I remember it, too."

"They met in September," I tell Perley now, "at an art exhibit. Mom won a prize. [There were a dozen artists in a hotel room. Mother's ink drawing of a sheep got honorable mention.] I was her assistant. ["I can't find anyone to baby-sit. I guess you'll have to come."] It was a catered affair. ["Don't get mustard on your clothes, Cyd. Try not to spill the soda pop."] I helped her set up canvases. ["Sit right there where I can keep an eye on you."] And advised prospective customers. ["Your mother's work is lovely, honey, but we want something blue to go with the carpet."] Daddy was giving a talk in the next room. After I finished helping Mom, I attended his lecture. ["Whose little girl is that? Where is that child's mother?"] His topic was industrial espionage. ["The first thing to consider when buying any piece of real estate is its location."] When he finished, he made a beeline to where I sat. ["Hey there, sugar, isn't it a bit late for you to be out on your own?"] I decided to introduce him to Mother. ["Excuse me, ma'am, is this your little girl?"] Mom was pleased to meet him. ["Thank goodness, I've been nearly frantic."] He insisted on accompanying us to the parking lot. ["Would you mind giving me a hand with these canvases?" Mother asked.] He offered to see us home. [Our car wouldn't start. "It's no trouble to drive you," he said.] Mother invited him up for dessert and a nightcap. [Instant coffee and melba toast were all that we had.] I think it was love at first sight," I tell Perley.

"What happened after that?" he wants to know.

"After that," I say, "they had a whirlwind courtship. It was wonderful. We dined out all the time ["Hamburgers and french fries are fine," Mother suggested nightly.], and went to the theater ["I like movies about dogs," Father insisted]. People stared at us wherever we went, we looked so happy. ["Is that your daddy?" strangers asked me. "Is that man over there your daddy?"]

"Thanksgiving that year we went to see the Macy's parade. I sat on Daddy's shoulders. I saw everything. [Also I got soaked. It rained all day, the turkey float collapsed, and Mother and I came home with colds. "Aunt Alice was the one," said Mother, "who always liked parades." She gave me hot tea with lemon. "It's good for your cold," she told me. I hate hot tea with lemon. "I feel exactly that way about parades," said Mother.]

"Christmas we visited Aunt Alice in her trailer in the country. We were snowed in by a blizzard. I got to sleep on an eiderdown mattress like the princess on a pea in the Hans Christian Andersen story. [It was cold in the trailer. I slept in a sleeping bag on the living room floor. Aunt Alice's three cats and the dog slept with me. The goat stayed in his shed. Mother slept with Aunt Alice, and Daddy got the extra bed. "It's because he's older," Mother told me. "She means taller," Daddy said. It's because I'm a girl, I thought at the time. "See," said Mother later, "you thought wrong."]

"They got married in the spring."

"Were you surprised?" asks Perley.

"Oh no," I say. "I knew it from the start. ["Are you going to marry him, Mom? Are you? Can I be flower girl if you do? Will he dance with me at the wedding?"] Well, maybe I was a little surprised. ["Cydra, we have something important to tell you. We just got married." "You're getting married?" I asked. "Is that what you said?" "Got," said Mother, "this morning." "But I was in school," I replied, sure that it mattered. "I've never even been to a wedding," I said. "How could you do it without me?" "We didn't have a wedding," Mother told me. "We only went to a judge. The courtroom was crowded, we waited in line, believe me, Cydra, you would have been bored." "I could have taken a book along and read it," I said. Mother sighed. "Can't you try to understand?" she said. "We just wanted to have lunch alone together after." "I see," I said.]"

"I don't see," says Perley, who has heard this all before

and knows it by heart, "why they didn't have a wedding and how come you weren't invited. You could have been Mom's flower girl."

"Well, sure," I agree, "but I was only five. Sometimes," I explain to my brother, "two people who are in love need to be alone, at least for lunch."

7

Shadows

I WAS fourteen and Perley was seven when Grandpa, our mother's father, died from complications of Parkinson's disease. He could no longer swallow. Unable to swallow, he couldn't eat. By then he'd had Parkinson's for nearly my whole life. Long before Perley had been born, Grandpa's once-steady doctor hands had started shaking. Then his head began to bob. Every time we saw him, he was worse. The medicine he took to ease his symptoms was powerless to cure. Increasingly it left him confused. Alice he would call my mother then. Alexis he would name Aunt Alice.

"Who cares?" said Mother. "It's only a name." She didn't care, and neither did Aunt Alice.

Toward the end it was hard for any of us to believe that the heart of a person who looked as he did could still go on beating. Each time I kissed him goodbye the thought almost froze me: Grandpa may die before I ever kiss him again.

"Can a ghost have Parkinson's?" Perley asked me once on the plane flying home from New York. He'd obviously given it some thought. I knew what he meant. I, too, had wondered. Sometimes I prayed that Grandpa wouldn't have to spend eternity the way he was.

"There's no such thing as a ghost," I heard myself explain to Perley. "Ghosts are only dead people we remember."

Grandpa died during Christmas recess. Perley and I and Mother were at Grandmother's house. Aunt Alice was with us. We took turns sitting in Grandpa's room by his side, watching him grow weaker. It was impossible the last few days for Grandpa to eat or drink or even take his medicine; still, we kept encouraging him to sip through a straw, anything. Propped up almost straight on borrowed pillows in the cranked-up hospital bed Grandma had rented, he looked like the death masks I had seen pictures of in Mother's art books. He held a plastic cup in his hand, just barely, and tried to sip beer through a straw. Mother and Aunt Alice discussed it in the kitchen.

"Eudora Welty's father once saved her mother's life," Mother informed Aunt Alice, "by giving her champagne." Eudora Welty is a famous writer. "It was before Eudora was born," she continued. "The doctors had given up hope. Eudora's mother couldn't swallow food, much less keep it down. Champagne couldn't be bought at that time in Jackson, Mississippi, which was where they lived. Eudora's father telephoned an Italian orchard grower forty miles north and begged him to put a bottle of number three wine on the Jackson train. When it arrived, chilled, Eudora's father gave it to her mother, who drank it, kept it down, and lived to tell the story." Mother related all of this as though it had a point.

Apparently it jogged Aunt Alice's memory. She recalled that Anton Chekhov, right before he died, had asked for champagne. Then, she said, he sat up in bed and drank it. Chekhov was a famous Russian writer, some of whose stories we'd read in school that fall. "He was also a physician," Aunt Alice emphasized. "Had your grandfather not been a doctor," she told Perley and me, "he might have been a writer. In Russia," she said, "he might have been both."

"He was a very good storyteller," Mother agreed, but when Perley asked her to tell one, she said she couldn't remember. Aunt Alice could.

"But he told them to me," Mother said, surprised. "You were always too little."

"Not always." Aunt Alice smiled. "When he told them to me, you were too big. You were always going out the door."

"Oh," said Mother, and sounded disappointed. Perley and I turned our attention to Aunt Alice.

"One time I asked him about shadows," she said. "They worried me the way they always came and went, taller and shorter, ahead and behind. They were so unreliable. I could never keep track of mine. Where did it come from? Where did it go?

"'Come from is easy,' Grandpa said. He told me about

the shadow maker, a tall, thin woman with smooth skin, straight teeth, and dark hair piled high onto her head. He said that she had three assistants who cut out the patterns that she drew, long and tall, fat and thin, shadows like people, shadows like dogs, fish shadows, eagle shadows, shadows of trees and clouds and mountains. Then the shadows were put into the world to watch. I asked him why my shadow wasn't always where I was. 'Sometimes even a shadow,' Grandpa explained, 'has to eat and sleep. In between is when it watches.'"

"Were you scared after that?" asked Perley.

"Oh no," Aunt Alice said. "I liked thinking of my shadow as a watcher. When I got older, he told me another story which was true. That one was scary." She told it to us.

Once it was the custom when a new graveyard was opened to bury a living person in the first grave to become a guardian over the cemetery. If a living person couldn't be found, then a shadow would have to do. The first one cast on the graveyard ground would be captured and covered quickly with dirt. The person whose shadow it was would die soon after and be buried there, too.

Sometimes it happened that way instead with a building. When a new structure wouldn't stand properly, the builders believed that its base required a man, or a woman, or a child, alive, whose skeleton could support the stone. When such a person couldn't be found, a shadow would be used. The shadow would be walled up with the stone, imprisoned in the mortar. Afterward, its owner would die.

I slept that night with Perley and Mother on blankets on the floor in Grandmother's living room. We hugged each other to keep warm. Aunt Alice slept alone in the only extra bed.

Naturally we didn't watch Grandpa every second all that week. When we didn't, a nurse's aide hired by Grandma did. Sometimes we went out, all of us or several at a time to eat. We ate in fast-food restaurants, ordered meals we barely touched, and wondered what to take back for whomever stayed behind. Some of those times, though we did not forget about Grandpa, we talked of other times. Once Perley asked Aunt Alice why she had never gotten married.

"You must have had chances," he said in his serious way.

"As a matter of fact," Aunt Alice replied, hiding a smile, "I had a chance just last summer. At the last minute I turned it down."

"Why did you do that?" asked Perley.

Though I tried not to show it, I, too, was interested in knowing. I myself have sometimes contemplated never getting married. "Like Aunt Alice," I once said to Mother, thinking of years of medical school and setting up a practice.

"Who ever said Aunt Alice was never getting married?" Mother asked, sounding surprised. "She just hasn't yet."

"Charles was the man in question," said Aunt Alice. "He was a lawyer. He was also an excellent cook, a great advantage, since, as you know, I'm not. I dated him for half a year. Charles had only one drawback so far as I could see. He was extremely fat."

Aunt Alice and Mother both are very slim. Aunt Alice is several inches taller. Though, unlike Mother, she pays infinite attention to her wardrobe, even a stranger could probably guess they were sisters. They have the same dark hair, pale skin, and extraordinary eyes—large, circular, and recessed. Their gestures and facial expressions are almost identical. "What nationality is your mother?" friends used to ask. "American," I'd tell them. "Yes," they'd agree, "but where is she from?" "She's from New York," I'd reply. "But where were her parents from?" they'd persist. "From Brooklyn; they used to live on Eastern Parkway, now they live in Manhattan." "Your mother looks Armenian," my best friend in fifth grade, Aspacious Beccataurus, finally decided. If she does, then so does my aunt Alice.

I watched her carefully as she poked at her food and continued her story. "While it's true," she said, "that I admire the principle behind slimness, I certainly wouldn't let a man's being fat stand in the way of romance. Charlie, however, insisted he wanted to be thin, and not only for my sake. He said his self-respect depended upon it. He told me he was on a diet. Though I never asked, he persisted in providing me with progress reports. 'I lost five pounds, I'm two sizes smaller,' he would say. I never noticed any difference, though I did realize from where he had started he had a long way to go and that a pound here or there might not be noticed right away. I tried to be encouraging. 'Wonderful,' I would tell him, utterly indifferent.

"One day on my way home from work I passed his apartment. I decided to surprise him and drop in. Was I ever surprised. The entire apartment, every room and corner, every nook and cranny, seemed to contain empty cartons, discarded boxes, opened bottles and depleted jars, crumpled cellophane bags, all of which had once held food, fattening food, food such as doughnuts, frozen pizza, ice cream, Milky Way bars, potato chips, and even Capt'n Crunch, for goodness' sake. No wonder Charlie was fat." Aunt Alice looked directly at Perley. "As far as I was concerned," she said, "that was that. Charles had lost whatever chance he might have had with me."

"Because he went off his diet?" Perley asked, incredulous. "You didn't marry him because of that?"

"I bet he was surprised. What did he say?" asked Mother, smiling the first time that week.

"He couldn't believe it," Aunt Alice told her. " 'You're acting as if you'd come up here and found another woman in my room instead of just an empty ice cream carton,' he told me. Well," she said, "I might as well have. A man who will lie about one thing will lie about another."

Mother laughed out loud then. "Grandpa always told us that," she said to me and Perley.

"Did he?" asked Aunt Alice. "Why don't I remember?"

"You were probably too young," said Mother, and looked pleased. Then she looked at her watch and sighed. We'd been out long enough; it was time to go back. It was always so hard to go back. We never knew what we'd find. It was hardest of all because we knew there was nothing we could do about it. We didn't know it. A visiting nurse came every day. Every day we waited, breaths drawn, for her to say, "This is a horrible mistake. This man belongs in a hospital." She never said it.

That day, when we got back, the nurse was there. She said, as she had said before, "You're doing everything that can be done."

I remembered years ago standing at my bedroom window, watching a tree uprooted by a storm; then I heard Aunt Alice saying in another room, "People walk on the moon." Like her, like all of us, I couldn't understand how this could be all that anyone could do.

"Why does he moan? Is he in pain?" Grandma asked the nurse softly.

The nurse didn't hear or else didn't know. She patted Grandma's arm. "You're doing fine," she told her.

The seventh day after we arrived Grandpa died, five minutes before midnight on Friday. His funeral was Sunday morning. "I hope that no one comes," said Mother, and almost no one did. Almost no one knew. Mother's family is extremely private.

When we were back home, I looked up the word "moan" in the dictionary: "A mournful sound of sorrow or of pain indicating unrelenting grief, more than one can bear."

The rest of that winter and the following spring I sometimes dreamed of Grandpa. I saw him propped on pillows in his bed and heard him moan in my sleep. The sound would waken me. Words are often used in error to say less than they mean, I'd think then, but once in a blue moon a word comes along that means exactly what it says. (A blue moon is when one month contains two full moons, according to my dictionary. It happens only once every few years. Why it is called a blue moon, though, is a mystery.)

I was not, of course, the only one that winter trying to adjust. Mother hardly ate and lost weight. When I looked at her drawing board, all the figures I saw there were skeletons. Perley walked in his sleep for the first time in over a year. Daddy, not knowing what to say to console us, was quieter than ever.

Grandma came to visit in the summer. She watched Mother pick at her food and looked at her sketches. Tact and patience are not among her strongpoints. "How stupid can you get?" She scolded her. "Do you think your father would have wanted you to starve? Alexis," she said more gently, "you must pull yourself together. It's bad for the children. It's on account of you that they can't sleep."

Her putting it that way seemed to restore some of Mother's perspective. She started eating more, and her drawings gradually took on flesh. They began to look normal. Nevertheless, weeks after Grandma had returned to New York, Mother expressed to me her feeling of imbalance. "It's as though the world were out of order all the time," she said. She told me about a story she'd read in which a man who was in his sixties mentioned that so many of his friends had recently died his address book had come to resemble a necropolis. He meant because he had to keep drawing lines through their names. A woman in

the story to whom he told this explained that in her address book she always used pencil. "Of course," said
Mother, "she meant she wrote the names in pencil so that
when their owners died, she could erase them. But the first
time I read it, I thought she meant she crossed them out in
pencil. Then, if it turned out they weren't really dead, she
only needed to rub out the lines in order to restore them."

I knew how Mother felt. Death's permanence continued
to elude me. Nor was she alone in seeking meaning in a
story. I recalled a folktale I once thought was pointless
about an exceptionally stupid girl named Else. She was
called Clever Else in the story.

When Clever Else was grown up, her father said, "It
is time to get her a husband."

Her mother agreed. "If only we can find someone
who'll have her."

At last a man who was named Hans came. He said
he would marry Else, but she had to be smart. "She has
common sense," said the father, "and more than
enough of that."

"She can see trouble coming up the street," said the
mother.

"Well," Hans said, "if that is the case, I will have
her, but if not, then I won't." So they sat down to
dinner.

Then the mother said, "Else, please go to the cellar
and fetch us some beer."

Clever Else took the pitcher from the wall. She went

down into the cellar, got a stool so as not to have to
stoop while she poured, placed the pitcher beneath the
tap, and turned it. While the beer was running, she
looked here and there until she saw a pickax hanging
just above her. It had been left there accidentally by the
masons when they worked. Else began to weep.

"Ah woe," she said. "Suppose I marry Hans and we
have a child, and when the child grows up, we send
him to the cellar to draw beer. He might sit right here
and the pickax fall on his head and kill him." So she sat
and wept while those upstairs waited for the ale. Finally
her mother sent a servant down to find out what was
keeping Else. The maid went and found Else weeping.

"Why do you weep?" asked the maid.

"Ah," Else answered, "as if I had not reason.
Suppose," she said, "I marry Hans and we have a
child, and he grows big and we send him to draw beer
and that pickax above us falls off the wall and kills
him."

Then the maid saw the way things were. "What a
Clever Else we have," she said, and sat down beside
her and wept loudly herself.

When the maid did not return and neither did Else
and there was no ale to drink, the man sent the boy.
"Just go down into the cellar," he told him, "and see
what can be keeping Else and the maid."

The boy went, and there sat Clever Else and the

maid, both weeping. "Why are you weeping?" he asked.

"Have we not reason?" they said.

"Suppose," said Else, "I marry Hans and we have a child and the child grows big and I send him to the cellar to draw beer. And what if that pickax falls on his head and kills him?"

"What a Clever Else we have," said the boy, and he began to howl.

Upstairs they waited. Finally the man sent his wife to the cellar. Down she went and found all three lamenting. She inquired as to the reason. When Else explained about the pickax, the mother saw the way things were, exclaimed, "What a Clever Else we have!" and sat down to cry with them.

The man upstairs was thirsty. When his wife did not come back, he went down into the cellar himself this time. When he saw them all sitting together crying and he heard the reason, he, too, exclaimed, "How clever our Else is!" sat down, and wept with them.

At last the intended bridegroom, tired of staying alone upstairs, thinking no one would ever come back and they must be waiting for him to join them, also went into the cellar. Seeing them crying, beer by now running everywhere on the floor, he asked, "What misfortune has befallen you?"

"Ah, dear Hans," said Else, "if we marry and have a child and he grows big and we send him to the cellar to

draw beer, the pickax up there may fall on his head
and kill him, and how can we not grieve at that?"

Then Hans saw how clever she was. He took her
hand and said, "Clever Else, indeed, I will have you."

They all went upstairs, a preacher was sent for, and
Hans and Else were married that day. No doubt they
lived happily ever after.

Whether or not they ever had a child, or sent him to the
cellar, or if a pickax fell on him and killed him, the story
doesn't tell us. What was clear to me, however, that hadn't
been clear before was how much cleverer than I Else was.
She knew right away, as I had not, that calamity is always
waiting just around a corner, and it can come exactly as a
pickax falling, unpredictably and with no warning, and
nothing anyone can do will change it. I thought about it
for some time; then I told it to my mother.

"Yes," she said. "But you do realize Else was clever
enough not to put off her wedding day waiting for that
pickax to fall. Life," she said, "is like that."

8 🦢

Dreams and
Memories

"DREAMS, I have heard it said, are the undersides of our days. Some even hold that dreams may be the world in which we live and that our daytime existence serves only to sustain us until night. Memories, I think, may be the border zone that links the night and day sides of our lives."

I wrote that in tenth grade in a journal which I kept. Sometimes I still keep it. I recalled it following a conversation Perley started at Aunt Sister's the first time we went back to visit after Granddad's heart attack.

Perley and I and some of our cousins were sitting on the floor in Tineen's room, talking. Mother, then Aunt Selena, and finally Aunt Sister joined us. First they sat to one side as though not wanting to intrude, then moved closer until we all formed a circle and took turns telling whatever occurred to us to tell.

It occurred to Perley to tell how he used to be afraid of monsters that lurked beneath his bed in the dark. "I thought if I could just keep my fingers and toes from hanging over the edges of the mattress while I slept that I'd be safe. Being afraid I'd forget used to keep me awake."

"Your dad used to be afraid of the dark," Aunt Sister told him. "So was your uncle William. When they had to get out of their beds at night for any reason, both of them put blankets on their heads."

"So they wouldn't see ghosts?" Perley asked.

"That, too," Aunt Sister said, "but mainly to scare away the ones they thought were out there."

"More than once," said Aunt Selena, "they scared me."

Aunt Selena, the youngest, is the one who hasn't finished school because she keeps on going. She owns and, when she isn't taking classes, operates an elegant boutique. She dresses in the latest fashion. She wears gold chains and silver bangles. I have seen her with acrylic nails. "What a beautiful face she has," my other grandmother said one time, examining her photograph. It is the sort of thing my grandmother says, willing to go so far and no farther with any compliment. I myself think Aunt Selena is beautiful period. Perley and my cousins think so, too.

She is tall with broad shoulders and perfect posture. She has a huge smile that is interrupted often when she moves her lips up and down and sideways to emphasize some point. She has eyes like Perley's, large and dark and fringed by lashes too long even for Aunt Selena to improve them by wearing fake ones. Beneath her left eye and to one side is a tiny beauty mark. Only her unpierced ears seem ordinary. All my girl cousins have holes in their lobes. Tineen has five, two in one and three in the other. "Why not put a ring through your nose?" Daddy asks whenever I beg for permission to have mine done.

Aunt Selena told what happened to a friend of hers when both of them were nine or ten.

"Dee," she said, "was very light-complexioned. One time, when her mother left her with a baby-sitter, an emergency came up and the sitter couldn't stay. She also couldn't take Dee with her, and she couldn't find a substitute to sit. Therefore, she took Dee downtown and put her on line outside the movie house. It was a white movie house. In our town," she explained, "there was a white theater and a black one. The white one had no balcony, so we were not allowed period. It was on the line to this theater that the sitter told Dee to wait. Heaven knows what she was thinking. When Dee got up to the ticket seller, she held up her dime. The woman peered down at her through the glass.

" 'What are you, sugar?' she asked. Dee looked up at the woman, then back at the line. It came to her what the woman meant. She swallowed hard and thought fast.

" 'Greek,' she said. 'I think I'm Greek.' " Aunt Selena laughed. "It was the first thing that came into her head, Dee told me later, though she never knew why. Neither one of us at that time so far as we knew had ever seen a person who was Greek. Probably the ticket seller hadn't either. She took Dee's dime and let her in.

"Years later," Aunt Selena continued, "I was on a college class trip. It was the beginning of integration. My class was black and white with a sprinkling of foreign students. The bus pulled up outside a restaurant, and we started to go in. The owner stopped us. 'We don't serve colored here,' he said. 'The white students are welcome.'

" 'Suppose,' the professor proposed, 'we line up from white to black in order of our color. We'll start coming, and you stop us when we get too dark.' "

"What happened?" Perley asked.

"The man was not amused," said Aunt Selena. "We got back on the bus and went someplace else where everyone could eat together standing up."

"That," said Aunt Sister, "was the in-between time called vertical integration. Some white people," she said, "who didn't care to sit down in the same rooms where black people did didn't mind standing up with them in integrated places. It was a joke that one could integrate the schools by removing the chairs. Well, we *thought* it was a joke until a public library in North Carolina was ordered by a federal court to integrate and the head librarian responded by taking out the seats.

"I remember being out in the country with Mother one time on a bus," she continued. "I kicked the seat in front of me. We sat in the first black row, so the seat I kicked was white. The driver stopped the bus and put us out. We walked miles to get home. I worried with every step I took what Mother would do to punish me when we got there. She didn't. She was too angry at the driver.

"Another time, though, it was a different story. We were at a county fair. Our car was pulled up to the fence the same as all the others. It was past sundown and nearly dark. A white man climbed onto our car hood so he could see better. He decided it would be fun to jump up and down. 'If I were you,' said Mother, 'I wouldn't do that anymore.' He grinned at her. Probably he'd been drinking. He kept on jumping. Mother got out her shotgun from the trunk. Those were the days she didn't drive anywhere, especially at night, without it. She pointed it at the man."

"What happened then?" Perley asked.

"The man stopped jumping on her car," Aunt Sister said. "He climbed down and went away."

The main difference between my two aunts, I thought as I watched and listened to them speak, was style. Aunt Sister's style is the opposite of Aunt Selena's. She wears plain clothes, rimless glasses, and hardly any makeup. She speaks softly, sits sedately, and looks like the college professor that she is. It struck me for the first time how she does not go with her large and fancy house, but then neither does Aunt Selena go with hers. She lives in a small apartment by herself.

"Almost the whole time I was growing up," Aunt Selena was saying, "I worried Daddy would get killed. Mother used to come home angry, at a bus driver or shopkeeper or stranger, for something that person had said to her or done. I was so afraid Daddy would do something about it and the police would come to the house and shoot him."

Reba, Cousin Billy's wife, Billy being Uncle William's son, remembered that when she was eight, she had almost gotten her brother killed. "He used to follow me everywhere," she said. " 'Stay home,' I used to tell him, but he would never listen. He followed me one day when I was on my way to a friend's house to play. I saw the car turning the corner as I started to cross the street. I hurried. I had just time enough to cross safely in front of it. I was sure my brother would have to turn around and go back home. Of course, he didn't. He was only five. He kept coming. So did the car. It was a miracle he wasn't killed. He spent a week in intensive care and the rest of that summer on crutches while his thighbone knit. The worst of it for me was that I was never punished."

The next memory was mine. When I was in kindergarten, my friend Philip was run over by a truck. He was trying to cross the street with his bicycle. He died in the hospital two days later. Though I was not allowed to cross any street alone, I worried a lot after that about dying. I worried especially about my mother's dying. She crossed streets alone all the time, and not always with the light. If she died, who would take care of me? My grandparents lived in an apartment that didn't allow children; no one under fourteen could live there permanently. My grandmother finally told me, "If your mother dies," as, she emphasized, was highly unlikely, "your grandfather and I are prepared to move so that you can come and live with us." I was greatly relieved to know it. "If I were you, though," Grandmother also told me, "I wouldn't mention it to your mother." I didn't, not then and not that evening at Aunt Sister's either. I kept my memory to myself.

"When I was little," I heard Tineen say, "I thought that when people died and were buried, they walked around underground at night in the cemetery, visiting. I used to worry I'd be buried among strangers, and there'd be no one for me to go see."

Mother remembered when she was little, her mother used a cleaning powder that had a picture on the label of a woman with a broom. "Dutch Cleanser," said Tineen. "It has a Dutch maid sweeping."

"Maybe," Mother said. "I used to dream at night that woman came and took away my sister, flew off with Alice on her broom. I'd wake up screaming. 'What's wrong with you?' My mother would scold me. 'Why can't you dream something pleasant?' What I've never understood," said Mother, "was why the dream upset me. It wasn't as if when we were growing up I got along that well with Alice."

After we left Aunt Sister's and were walking back to Grandmother's, which was where we spent the night, Mother told me one more memory. Perley had walked ahead with Daddy; they were holding hands, swinging arms.

"The summer I was seven," Mother said, "and Aunt Alice was a baby, Grandma and Grandpa took us on a trip to Florida by car. It was quite an adventure. I saw wheat-fields, cotton in bloom, and cows grazing all for the first time. Grandpa stopped at nearly every ice cream stand and bought us all banana ice cream cones. We stopped at a department store in Georgia so Grandma could buy something she needed for Alice. Grandpa and I wandered into the hardware section. Along one wall were two water fountains. There was a sign over each. One said 'white,' the other said 'colored.' I read them several times, trying to decide what they meant. Finally I decided. Regular water must come from the white one, and colored water from the other. I had experience after all. Grandpa had a collection of antique apothecary jars at home, some of which could be illuminated. They were filled with colored water. I pictured a rainbow coming from the colored fountain. I went to drink from it. As I was about to turn the knob, a woman came up behind me. 'You want that one,' she told me, pointing. That quickly, I knew what those signs meant. I looked around for Grandpa. He was several aisles away. If he had seen what just transpired, he gave no sign. For the rest of our trip I watched for them, for signs outside rest rooms, motel signs, water fountain signs, signs to show that grown-ups saw the signs I did. I never discussed it with Grandpa, but my early confidence in his ability to make every wrong thing right had been permanently eroded. Afterward I always knew some things were beyond him."

Going home in the car next day, Perley asked Daddy about dreams. "Tell us one of yours," he said.

"Engineers don't dream," Daddy answered with a straight face. "I know of a peddler, though, who did," he said, and told us this story:

Once there was a peddler who had hardly anything at all to his name except for the hut in which he lived, the land on which it stood, and the pots and the pans that he peddled. He had a dream, though. He dreamed one night that if he walked from Durham Town, where he lived, to the next big city and crossed the bridge, he'd find his fortune. So he did it. It took him three days and three nights walking, but when he'd crossed the bridge, he found no fortune. The peddler was patient, though, and waited. He walked back and forth on the bridge all day and slept on the hard, cold ground at night. The bridgekeeper became curious. After several days had passed, he asked the peddler, "Who are you and what are you doing here?"

The peddler explained. "I dreamed," he said, "if I crossed this bridge, I'd find my fortune. I walked three days and nights from Durham Town to get here, but I haven't found it yet." The bridgekeeper laughed at the peddler. "Why, just the other night," he said, "I dreamed if I left here and went to that place you say you're from and dug beneath a pecan tree behind some peddler's hut, I'd find a treasure. But you don't see me running off, do you?"

"You're right," the peddler said, "I don't." He tried to hide his pleasure, but as soon as the bridgekeeper went back to his station, the peddler packed up his wares and set off for home. It took him only two days and two nights to get there, for now he walked much faster than he had before. He knew just the tree that bridgekeeper had dreamed about. When he got home, he took a shovel, went behind his hut, and dug beneath the pecan tree that stood in his backyard. And sure enough, he found a treasure. With it he bought a fine new house, and clothes, a wagon for his pots and pans, and a mule to pull the wagon. So far as I know, he lived happily ever after.

Daddy looked at me. "So did the mule," he said.

Several weeks later Perley woke me in the middle of the night to tell me his dream. This was what he told me.

"I dreamed," he said, "I was myself, but I thought I was a chicken. I took my clothing off, put on some feathers, and climbed underneath the kitchen table. The only food that I would eat was corn seed, which I pecked from the floor. After some time had passed, Granddad came back from being dead and joined me. He, too, had taken off his clothes and had on feathers. He was pecking corn seed from the floor. 'Who are you, and what are you doing here?' I asked him in my dream.

" 'Who are you,' he asked me back, 'and what are you doing here?'

" 'I'm a chicken,' I explained. 'I'm eating my dinner.'

" 'Really,' he said, 'well, so am I.' Some time went by. Granddad called for his clothes to be brought and exchanged his feathers for them. I looked at him suspiciously. He looked at me back and said, 'Just because one is a chicken doesn't mean he can't dress as he likes. A chicken can wear a suit and tie and still be a very fine chicken.' I thought about it, and then I, too, exchanged my feathers for my clothing. More time passed. Granddad called for regular food to be brought to him. I watched as he ate it. He watched me back. 'Don't think,' he said, 'because one is a chicken, he cannot eat as he likes. A chicken can eat the same as a person and still be a very fine chicken.' After I thought about it for a while, I, too, began to eat his food. Finally Granddad came out from beneath the table and began to walk about in the kitchen. I watched him. He said to me, 'Don't think because one is a chicken, he cannot walk about as he likes. A chicken can go anywhere and still remain a chicken.' Well, I thought that over, too, and decided he was right. I came out from beneath the table and began to walk about in the kitchen. After some more time had passed and I had been eating as a person, dressing as a person, and walking about as a person, I began to think I was a person. That was when I woke up."

"I like your dream," I told him.

"Yes," he said, close to tears, "except that Granddad's dead. What can it mean?"

I tried hard to think of something helpful to tell him. I remembered about Clever Else and what Mother had told me. "I think what it means is this," I said to Perley. "Life as a person is hard, but it's better by a long shot than being a chicken." Perley seemed satisfied with my interpretation. I, however, am not that positive about it anymore. It occurred to me not long afterward to check out Mother's brand of cleaning powder. She buys Bon Ami. You can imagine how surprised I was to see a picture of a chicken on its label.

9 ☙

American History

JUST as I began believing this household was settling down to normal after Granddad's death, Daddy started acting strange. Our home became a history lesson, and Daddy a historian. When I tried to pinpoint the precise beginning, I remembered one evening after dinner Daddy's reading to us from a magazine. I think it was the black writer Alice Childress whom he quoted recalling public school when she was growing up in Harlem: "'Africa is coming up tomorrow,' we used to warn each other. 'Did you get a look at page 87 in the social studies book? I ain't going back to school, girl, until Africa is over.'"

Daddy, of course, had gone to private black schools in the South. He'd never had to learn and then repeat for tests how Africans had liked picking cotton in the South, were accustomed to hot weather, grateful for having been brought to America in chains, saved from their homeland. The next morning we found a list in the kitchen he had taped to the wall. It turned out to be the first of many.

Africa:

- Is the second-largest continent.
- It is four times the size of the United States.
- It is three times the size of Europe.
- Human beings are believed to have originated in Africa.
- The first tools they ever used they used in Uganda.
- Over eight thousand years ago the Ishongo people had an abacus of sorts, possibly the oldest multiplication table ever used in the world. It was used in what is now called the Congo.
- Iron smelting likely began in Africa, then spread to Europe and Asia.
- All competitive ball and bat games, including baseball, including tennis, can be traced to Egypt, a country in Africa, where they were practiced as part of religious rites around 1500 B.C.
- By A.D. 1000, before Columbus was born, much less landed in the Americas, Ghana was a kingdom with broad streets, stone buildings, utensils of silver and gold.
- Within the same decade that Columbus made his famous first trip, the University of Sankore, in Africa, had become a center of intellectual life; scholars came from Europe and Asia to study law, surgery, history, and literature. Important academic centers existed at Timbuktu, at Gao, at Walata, and at Jenné.

Several days later another list was taped beside it, information about the role of black people in American history. I already knew that black explorers had sailed with Columbus, accompanied Balboa, traversed the continent, that black soldiers had defended America in every war, but some of it I hadn't heard before.

"I didn't know that," said Perley, who in fourth grade was immersed in the American Revolution. His history books lay open on his desk. Naturally Crispus Attucks, Peter Salem, and Benjamin Banneker were mentioned in them. Perley compared the illustrations in his books with Daddy's list. Black colonists, he read, participated in the Stamp Act riots, were Green Mountain Boys, were Minutemen whom Paul Revere alerted, had wintered at Valley Forge and crossed the Delaware with Washington. A person couldn't have known it from looking at the pictures. Perley got out his crayons and began to color them in.

"What are you doing?" I asked.

"I'm editing," he explained.

I wondered what Mother would say if she saw, but then I considered how she'd been the one to teach us both to capitalize neatly the *N* in "Negro" anyplace we saw it wrong, even in a textbook.

"Why is Daddy doing this?" I asked Mother after his third list had gone up. It was headed "Historic Black Americans."

"It's probably his way of adjusting," she told me. "He misses Granddad terribly. I think he is only now beginning to believe he's really gone." Then I remembered all the skeletons my mother drew three years ago.

Predominant on Daddy's newest list were scientists and inventors. I was not surprised. He is, after all, an engineer himself. Perley and I took turns reading aloud to each other about Norbert Rillieux, born a slave in Louisiana, whose invention of the vacuum evaporation pan revolutionized the process of refining sugar around the world; Lewis H. Latimer, associate of Thomas Edison and Alexander Graham Bell, holder of numerous patents for electric lighting systems; Jan E. Matzeliger, whose invention for attaching shoe uppers to soles by machine revolutionized the shoemaking industry and gave the United States international supremacy in it; Granville T. Woods, holder of more than fifty patents, whose inventions included the egg hatchery incubator, the third rail, which allowed electricity to replace steam on elevated railways, and systems for transmitting messages between moving trains and between moving trains and stations. Perley's favorite was Frederick McKinley Jones, who went to school only four years but mastered electronics, physics, and mechanics. Frederick Jones was awarded more than sixty patents, including those for portable X-ray machines, refrigeration equipment, and the ticket dispenser used by movie theaters. The part of the list that interested me most was about the physicians. Some of their names I copied down in my journal.

I put down James Derham, first black physician in America, who'd been born a slave in Philadelphia in 1762; and Cesar, a nineteenth-century medical practitioner, born a slave, but given his freedom by the South Carolina General Assembly out of gratitude for his discovery of a treatment for rattlesnake bite. I added Daniel Hale Williams, famous for being first in the world to perform a successful operation on the human heart (July 9, 1893, at Providence Hospital in Chicago, a hospital he founded), and Charles Richard Drew, whose blood plasma research allowed establishment of blood banks and large-scale transfusion and saved countless lives during and after World War II.

I gave the most space, however, and liked best to know about the women. There were so many of them. By the end of just the 1800s there were 160 black female physicians in the United States. The first woman doctor in many states had been a black woman doctor. There was Halle Tanner Dillon Johnson, first woman doctor in Alabama; Verina Harris Morton Jones, first woman doctor in Mississippi; Matilda Arabella Evans, first woman doctor in South Carolina; Sarah Boyd Jones, first woman doctor in Virginia. There were too many names to list them all.

"Why is Daddy doing this?" Perley asked me as I had asked Mother.

"It's just a stage," I explained to him. "A stage of mourning. We have to be patient." I recalled stages I'd been through and Daddy's patience. "You'll see," I said, trying to sound reassuring. "He'll adjust and be himself again."

It turned out I was both right and wrong. More lists went up. Perley and I learned that the first Jim Crow railroad car had gone into service in 1841, in Massachusetts. Also that year, school districts in New York State were given the right to segregate; black and white millhands in South Carolina were forbidden to look out the same windows; whites and blacks in Atlanta had to swear on different Bibles in court. Black streetcar riders could ride only streetcars in New York City which bore a banner on either side, "Colored People Allowed in This Car." Eventually Florida required "Negro" and "white" textbooks to be segregated in warehouses, and Oklahoma, in 1915, required "separate but equal" phone booths; "Negroes" had to be off the streets by 10:00 P.M. in Mobile, Alabama, and blacks and whites were forbidden by law to play checkers together in Birmingham.

"Are you angry?" Perley asked Daddy at dinner that night.

"Angry?" Daddy answered. "Why should I be angry?"

He didn't sound especially angry, but I was not convinced. Angry at whom, though? I wondered. After dinner I did the dishes with my mother. "How long do you think it will take," I asked, "for Daddy to adjust?"

She shrugged. "Everyone is different; we just have to give him time," she answered.

"I'd be angry," Perley said the next day, showing me a list of his own. He was not a person to equivocate, so his was simply headed "Lynching." It included the following information: Between 1890 and 1900 there were 1,217 mob murders by hanging, burning, shooting, or beating recorded in the United States. There were 114 lynchings reported in newspapers from January to October 1900. Between 1918 and 1921, 28 human beings were publicly burned at the stake in America. "There have been no recorded lynchings in this country since 1968," he told me.

When I did not seem as responsive to his news as he apparently had expected me to be, he told me about Ida B. Wells Barnett. "She was a woman," he said, in case I missed his point. "She was a black woman, a journalist; a crusader for an antilynch law. She walked the streets of Memphis," he read from his notes, "with two guns strapped to her waist. Don't you want to know why?" He prodded me as I sat trying to absorb his figures.

"Why?" I asked automatically.

"For a black woman who spoke out against lynching, it was the only safe way," he answered, a note of triumph in his voice. "Are you going to put her in your journal?" he asked.

I added her name after my list of women physicians.

Days passed, and weeks. More lists followed, lists of famous black performers, musicians, composers, athletes, painters, writers, politicians. Daddy's lists covered the kitchen walls. Nor were lists all. He brought home books for us to read, novels, histories, poetry. He recited famous lines he'd memorized in school, by Langston Hughes, Paul Laurence Dunbar, James Weldon Johnson, and others. Then, almost as abruptly as it started, his propensity for lists subsided. The last one I recall was headed "Proverbs, African." The ones I liked best I wrote in my notebook, a few I learned by heart.

· When you follow in the path of your father, you learn to walk like him (*Ashanti*).

- He who asks questions cannot avoid the answers (*Cameroon*).
- Quarrels end, but words once spoken never die (*Sierra Leone*).
- No matter how long the winter, spring is sure to follow (*Guinea*).
- He who does not know one thing knows another (*Ivory Coast*).

Then, one day before the end of summer, all the lists were gone. "It must mean," Perley said, "that Daddy has adjusted." I looked up the word. "Adjust," according to my dictionary, means to alter so as to fit. I thought about it. I guessed we'd all adjusted. I guessed we had to. I envisioned a family as stars in the sky. When one member died, it was as though a star had gone out. It left a black hole. I saw stars shifting, altering their arrangement, trying hard to realign themselves to fit an unknown plan. I thought of my parents. I looked at Perley. I considered myself. Another of Daddy's proverbs came to my mind, from Tanganyika: "One does not cross a river without getting wet."

The history which Daddy had fastened to the kitchen walls was taken down but not forgotten. It became something we knew and kept on knowing. As Perley and I got older, we sought to keep it in perspective and understand it better. When I went to college, I took a course in American history as an elective, to fulfill a liberal arts requirement for premed students. "Take it; it's a snap," we told each other. "It's four years of high school history one more time." It turned out we were wrong. The professor, Dr. Dixon, was black, a woman, and American. What she taught was news to my classmates. "It isn't fair," they complained to each other. I recalled my father's lists and heard him say, "The slave trade lasted nearly four hundred years. It transported fifteen million slaves and cost the lives of some forty million Africans. Why is that so seldom put in textbooks?" Fair, I saw, was relative.

10 🐘
Thanksgiving

EVERY Thanksgiving since Mother and Daddy were married we have spent in Virginia at Grandmother's house surrounded by relatives. Nevertheless, if Perley or I ask in October, as we always do, "Where are we going for Thanksgiving?" nobody knows. "Are we going to Grandmother's?" We persist. "We'll see," our parents answer. They seem to be the only ones uncertain. Our mother's side of the family has no doubts.

"I suppose," Aunt Alice will say, making her own plans, "you'll be in Virginia as always."

"I assume," Grandma says from New York, "you'll be at your father's parents' for Thanksgiving."

"Probably," we tell them. "We're not absolutely positive."

"Ummmm," they reply, unimpressed.

There is no point in Perley or my taking personally this lack of information. Mother probably knows no more than we do, and Daddy is only following a family tradition. In this family, as any cousin could inform you every bit as well as I, it is useless questioning the grown-ups. They do not give straight answers. "Come go with me" is a joke among the children. When I was younger, I used to think it was only Daddy. "Go where?" I would ask. "How long will we stay? What time are we coming back?" "We'll see," he'd say. I learned early never to leave without a book and, if I could help it, a chocolate bar as well.

Cousin to cousin, growing older, we compared notes. "Will we be that way when we're grown-up?" we asked each other, disbelieving. "I won't," Perley insisted with confidence. But I have noticed already that Aunt Sister's oldest children, Mattie and P.C., cannot be counted on to tell their plans. "Will they be here this Thanksgiving?" I asked last year, but nobody knew until they turned up. Mattie didn't turn up until the next day. "We weren't sure you were coming," everyone said. "It's impossible," she explained, "to get an airplane reservation on Thanksgiving." "Especially," Tineen pointed out, "if you haven't decided until the night before." "What I always do," Aunt Selena said, "is make several and hold on to them until I make up my mind." Mother's face registered her surprise.

They don't behave this way just with children either. Even among themselves, they keep their plans a secret. "That way," I once heard Daddy explain to Mother, "no one else is inconvenienced if I have to change them." It reminded me of Aunt Alice's frequently complaining about how Grandmother never told anyone when there was a problem. "There's no point in worrying everyone," Grandma says. "Therefore," says Aunt Alice, "we're worried all the time."

It continues to be a source of amazement to Perley and me, and all of our cousins as well, how all of them, or even some of them, ever get together in one place at one time. That they have managed to do so every Thanksgiving for all of their lives can be considered nothing short of a miracle. Like homing pigeons, Perley pointed out last year.

None of the children, given a choice, would miss the trip. "Thanksgiving at Grandmother's is the same as in the movies," Tineen says every year. "It's like television," Perley concurs, probably thinking of John Boy on Walton's Mountain, where everyone is poor in money but rich in love, children are plentiful, they all get along and sing songs. Well, it's true that we always sing songs on Thanksgiving.

Uncle William plays Grandmother's organ, and we stand in a half circle around him. He plays such tunes as "Rock of Ages, cleft for me,/Let me hide myself in Thee," or "Amazing grace, how sweet the sound," or "Yes, we'll gather at the riv-er,/The beau-ti-ful, the beau-ti-ful riv-er." He also plays other songs, "Go Tell Aunt Rho-die," or "The Rock Is-land Line is a might-y good road,—Oh, the Rock Is-land Line is the road to ride," or Perley's favorite, "Turkey in the Straw," with Perley leading us in the chicken chorus Granddad taught him: "Oh, I had a little chicken and she wouldn't lay an egg/So I poured hot water up and down her leg/And the little chicken cried/And the little chicken begged/And the goshdarn chicken laid a hard-boiled egg." Sometimes this reminds Perley of his favorite chicken story, which he then proceeds to tell us. It's about the devil and a deal he once made with the chicken. It seems the devil offered the chicken one thing for each feather the chicken would trade him. In the end the chicken gave up all its feathers and died. It got cold. Perley heard the story in Sunday school.

Mother stands alongside us at the organ, but she doesn't sing. "I would if I could," she says when pressed. She believes she has no talent for music and doesn't mean only singing or playing it. When others clap their hands or tap their feet, Mother's face assumes an unnatural stiffness, and something in her posture makes you think she's sitting on her hands even when she's standing. Of course she's not. Her hands most likely are clasped together or crossed at chest level and tucked behind her elbows as though she were afraid they might get away from her.

"In my next life," she has said to whomever will listen, "I plan to play an instrument." It may be she feels the lack especially because she comes from a talented family. Her parents both were excellent musicians, and several of her uncles on either side played for a living. Only she and Aunt Alice seem unable to learn even so little as clapping in rhythm. "I think it's a talent one has to inherit," Mother has said in her long-suffering tone.

"What talent did you inherit?" I asked her once.

"Painting is a talent." She sighed. "Poetry is a form of art. My father's grandmother was a poet," she went on. "She wrote in Serbo-Croatian, however, which the children never learned to read. Therefore, they didn't save her poems. Also, there was a great-aunt who I am told drew lovely pencil sketches. Unfortunately they all fell overboard when she was coming to America, and afterward she never had the heart to start again."

The first Thanksgiving together after Granddad died turned out a bit of a surprise. For one thing, Grandmother didn't come. Daddy drove right past her house and stopped the car outside Aunt Selena's. We piled out and went inside.

"Hi, baby. Hi, sugar," Aunt Selena said as she hugged and kissed us indiscriminately. Her face was flushed from the hot stove in which a ham was baking. Aunt Sister, she explained, was bringing the turkey and yams, and Uncle William had promised to pick up a half dozen sweet potato pies on his way. Her apartment was already crowded with relatives and friends.

"Where's Grandmother?" Perley finally asked, saving me having to.

"Grandmother," Aunt Sister explained, having arrived by then with a roasted turkey large enough that Daddy had to help Uncle Phillip carry it in from the car, "is in Africa. She went to Senegal," she added as though in itself that explained it. Had she said the moon, I couldn't have been much more surprised. Mother and Perley looked as amazed as I. Since Daddy's expression never changed, I assumed that he already knew.

"So," I asked, after Daddy said grace and we were all eating, "what made Grandmother decide to go to Senegal? I mean," I added, not wanting to be misunderstood, "why not Kenya or Uganda?" I am not one of those people who believe that traveling abroad means going only to Europe. Myself I've always dreamed of the Orient. I used to seek out books that told of Marco Polo.

"I think," Aunt Sister explained, offering me more yams, "that it was cheaper."

"Oh," I said, putting more food in my mouth. I didn't ask, Cheaper than what?

"Cheaper than what?" Mother asked Daddy later, driving home.

He smiled mysteriously. "You can ask her yourself," he replied. "We're picking her up next Friday at the airport. She's landing in D.C."

"So," I asked on Friday as we waited for Grandmother's baggage to come off the plane, "how was Africa?"

"Nice," she said. "Senegal was very interesting."

She brought back presents. Mother got a scarf, Daddy some coins, and Perley a puppet. I got a necklace. It was strung with brown gourds, red and yellow beads and seeds, and multicolored pods. "If you prefer," Grandmother offered, "you can give me back the necklace, and I will trade you some silver bangles for it." I told her no. I preferred keeping what I had. Bangles, I thought, could be gotten anywhere, but an African necklace was something to own.

"How did you happen to choose Senegal?" I asked.

"I got a very good price for one thing," she said. "Also, Senegal is such a nice name. I like the way it just rolls off the tongue." She didn't say anything more for a few minutes. Then she said, "I thought of Thanksgiving with

Granddad gone. I couldn't see spending it here this year without him." She closed her eyes, then opened them. "When I was coming along, the grown-ups used to tell a story about flying. They said some Africans could do it. They said when things got too bad, there were slaves who put down their spades and their hoes, stood straight in the fields in the sun, and grew wings where their shoulder blades were. Then, just like that, they flew back to Africa. Of course, white people in those days tried to keep it quiet. They worried it could become contagious. I decided to go see for myself about that story. I bought a ticket and flew back to where folks came from." She leaned back in her chair. "It was nice to go; now it's nice to be back home."

That night I dreamed that I could fly. I was wearing my baby ring in the dream. It was by turning the ring on my finger that I acquired the ability to do it. When I woke up, though the details of the dream eluded me, I recalled the ring. It was gold, set with a tiny sapphire. It had belonged to Aunt Alice when she was a girl. She had given it to me. I used to insist on wearing it even to sleep. "It will cut off your circulation," Mother warned. "You'll wake up one morning with only nine fingers." Eventually I outgrew the ring, and Mother put it away. "You can have it back when you're older," she said. "You may want to wear it on a chain around your neck or save it for when you have a daughter."

The day after my dream I asked Mother for my ring back. "I want to wear it on Grandmother's necklace," I explained.

"Be careful you don't lose it," she said as she got it out of her trunk for me. "It's an interesting thing about that ring," she told me. "When your aunt Alice and I were small, she used to wear it to bed, the same way that you did. Grandmother warned her about cutting off her circulation the same way I warned you. But she was just as stubborn. She used to tell me that if she turned the ring on her finger a certain way in the night, a horse would come, a horse with wings, and take her on a journey. Naturally," said Mother, "being older, I didn't believe her. But she made it sound so convincing that even knowing better, I would beg her to take me along on one of her trips. Sometimes she promised that one night she would, usually in exchange for some favor from me, but she never did. Well, of course, I knew it was only a story, but still I pestered Grandma for a ring like Alice's. You have a bracelet, Grandma would remind me. She believed to give sisters everything alike risked spoiling them. Evening after evening," Mother concluded, "I wore my bracelet to bed and turned it in the night. But there was no magic in it, and I never got to fly." She handed me the ring.

I was too surprised by her story to say anything, much less tell her about my dream or Grandmother's story of flying Africans. I did sleep that night wearing both the necklace and the ring. Of course, nothing came of it. I hadn't really thought anything would.

When I woke up, however, Perley was leaning over me, staring into my face. "What do you think you're doing?" I asked. Actually I knew. He had listened to Mother's story, too. "I didn't fly if that's what you think," I told him.

"Of course you didn't," he said. "People don't fly. What did you dream about?"

"I didn't," I replied, and that was the truth.

"Everybody dreams," he informed me. "It's a scientific fact. Sometimes they just forget when they wake up."

"Well, then," I said, "I just forgot."

Before Christmas I saw Grandmother again. I was wearing my necklace. "It looks nice," she said, smiling. "You know, Cydra, flying to Africa makes an interesting story, but the world is bigger than just Senegal. I'm thinking of going to China next year. How would you like to join me, along with your cousin Tineen? It would be your graduation present. Also," she added, "you both could help carry my luggage."

I was almost speechless. I could hardly believe it. "I'd love it," I told her.

That night I told Perley the only Chinese story I remembered. It was about a farm girl who wanted to grow wings.

"She lived with her granddad," I told him, "and looked after the chickens. She wanted a pair of wings in order to fly. One warm spring day she stood in the yard and flapped her arms up and down, hoping to grow some. The daughter of the man who owned the land saw her.

" 'What are you doing?' she asked.

" 'Growing wings,' said the farm girl. 'I'm going to fly.'

"When the landowner's daughter heard that, she wanted wings also. If the girl who only looked after chickens could hope to grow some, certainly her own chances were much better, she thought. So she sprinkled her shoulders with water, thinking that water generally helped things to grow, then stood in the sun and flapped her arms up and down, too. The merchant's daughter passed by.

" 'What are you doing?' she asked.

" 'Growing wings,' said the landowner's daughter. 'I'm going to fly.' She explained about the farm girl.

"The merchant's daughter doubled over with laughter. Country people, she thought, are so foolish. But back in the city she reflected. If it won't help, it can't hurt, she told herself, and rubbed olive oil on her shoulder blades. Then she went to stand in the sunshine and wave her arms to see if wings would sprout.

"The magistrate's daughter saw her.

" 'What are you doing?' she asked.

" 'Growing wings,' replied the merchant's daughter. 'I'm going to fly.' She told about the farm girl and the landowner's daughter.

" 'Growing wings,' said the magistrate's daughter, 'is only for aristocrats.' She went home and took a soybean milk bath, then went out-of-doors and waited patiently for wings to grow.

"Not long after, the princess passed by with her royal retinue and saw the magistrate's daughter waving her arms up and down in the sun. She sent a messenger to find out what the girl was doing. The messenger came back and told the princess what the girl had said about the other girls and growing wings and how to do it.

" 'They're wasting their time,' said the princess. 'Wings are just for royalty.' Back at the castle she sprinkled rice wine on her shoulders, stood on her balcony, and flapped her arms.

"Her mother, the queen, saw her and asked, 'What do you think you're doing?' The princess explained about the wings. Naturally the queen did not believe it. Still, she thought, a fine thing it would be if my daughter should fly before I do. So she sprinkled her own shoulders with her finest perfume and stood where she hoped that she wouldn't be seen and practiced trying to fly just in case it should be true.

"Pretty soon, as you might imagine, all over China girls and women of every background were standing outside, waving their arms up and down in the sun. No work was getting done. The men were frantic.

"The Spirit in Charge of Wings heard about what was going on. She flew down to see for herself. If I give them all wings, she thought, they'll spend all their time flying. Who will look after the babies?

"I will give only one pair of wings, she decided, and I will give it to the one who thought of it first.

"So that was how the farm girl got her wings and afterward could fly wherever she liked, and all the other children and grown-ups in China went back to doing what they'd always done."

"It's a good story," said Perley. "It's a lot like Aunt Alice's dream."

"It is?" I didn't see much similarity myself.

"Well sure." He explained. "There are chickens in it instead of a horse, and the girl dreams by day instead of by night, but the moral is the same."

"Perley," I asked, "exactly what do you think is the moral?"

"The moral," he told me patiently, "is that just because a person has a dream doesn't mean that it won't happen."

It sounded to me more like a proverb he had made up than a moral, but I was not inclined to pursue it. I was already planning my trip to China in my head. Besides, for all I knew, proverb making ran in the family. Daddy's most recent was right that minute affixed to the hallway mirror: "There is no bridge until a person first imagines crossing the river." And Granddad had ended more than one story with "Chickens have wings, but you don't see them fly, do you?"

Later I would think about it and come to see what Perley meant. A person could soar without ever leaving the ground. The right story, and not a pair of wings, is the first prerequisite of flight. I wrote it in my journal.

SOURCES

THE events in this book are fiction, and the characters imagined, with the following exceptions:

The information about the creation of Coca-Cola attributed to the writer Alice Walker in Chapter 3 is from an essay by her on "China" published in *Ms.* magazine (March 1985).

The story about Snake, which Cydra tells in Chapter 4, is a folktale from Ghana and may be found in many collections of African stories.

The story about Eudora Welty's parents in Chapter 7 is based on information contained in *One Writer's Beginnings* by Eudora Welty (Cambridge, Mass.: Harvard University Press, 1984). The graveyard watcher mentioned in Chapter 7 appears in ghost stories throughout Europe; it is called an Ankou. The idea of an address book as a necropolis in that same chapter was borrowed from a story, "The Dragon," by Muriel Spark in the *New Yorker* (August 12, 1985). "Clever Else," which concludes Chapter 7, was adapted from the Grimm Brothers' tale of the same name; many variations of the tale can be found in many cultures.

The story about the peddler told by Cydra's father in Chapter 8 is based on the old English folktale "The Pedlar of Swaffham," which can be found in its traditional form and with notes in *English Fairy Tales,* collected, annotated, and introduced by Joseph Jacobs (Bodley Head, Ltd., 1968). Perley's dream about being a chicken, which concludes Chapter 8, is based on the Jewish story "The Prince Who Thought He Was a Rooster," by Rabbi Nachman of Bratslav, retold from the Yiddish and Hebrew sources by Jack Reimer in *Gates to the New City: A Treasury of Modern Jewish Tales,* edited and with an introduction by Howard Schwartz (New York: Avon Books, 1983).

Historical information presented in Chapter 9 came from a wide range of sources. Principal among them were: *Before the Mayflower: A History of the Negro in America, 1619–1964,* revised edition, by Lerone Bennett, Jr. (Chicago: Johnson Publishing Company, 1964); *The Negro Almanac: A Reference Work on the Afro-American,* fourth edition, compiled and edited by Harry A. Ploski and James Williams (New York: John Wiley & Sons, 1983); and *The Shaping of Black America,* by Lerone Bennett, Jr., (Chicago: Johnson Publishing Company, 1975). The proverbs are from the book *African Proverbs,* compiled by Charlotte and Wolf Leslau (White Plains, N.Y.: Peter Pauper Press, 1962). The information on black women doctors came principally from *We Are Your Sisters: Black Women in the Nineteenth Century,* edited by Dorothy Sterling (New York: W. W. Norton & Company, 1984).

The Sunday school story in Chapter 10 about the devil and the chicken was told by Denise Dixon in the book *Portraits and Dreams, Photographs and Stories by Children of the Appalachians*, edited by Wendy Ewald (New York: Writers and Readers Publishing, Inc., 1985). The story in that same chapter of Africans who could fly is well known and variously told. The story about growing wings that concludes the book was adapted from "Growing Wings" in *The Milky Way and Other Chinese Folk Tales* by Adet Lin (New York: Harcourt, Brace & World, Inc., 1961). It was published earlier in *Erh Tung Shih Chieh* magazine, Vol. 18, No. 3 (1926).